PRA

Scream Catcher

"Sensational . . . masterful . . . brilliant."

—*New York Post*

"My fear level rose with this Zandri novel like it hasn't done before. Wondering what the killer had in store for Jude and seeing the ending, well, this is one book that will be with me for a long time to come!"

—*Reviews by Molly*

"I very highly recommend this book . . . It's a great crime drama that is full of action and intense suspense, along with some great twists . . . Vincent Zandri has become a huge name and just keeps pouring out one best seller after another."

—*Life in Review*

"A thriller that has depth and substance, wickedness and compassion."

—*The Times-Union (Albany)*

"I also sat on the edge of my seat reading about Jude trying to stay alive when he was thrown into one of those games . . . Add to that having to disarm a bomb for good measure!"

—*Telly Says*

The Disappearance of Grace

"The Disappearance of Grace is a gripping psychological thriller that will keep you riveted on the edge of your seat as you turn the pages."

—*Jersey Girl Book Reviews*

"This book is truly haunting and will stay with you long after you have closed the covers."

—*Beth C., Amazon 5-star review*

MOONLIGHT SONATA

Vincent Zandri

StoneGate Ink 2013
Boise ID 83713
http://www.stonegateink.com

First eBook edition: 2013
First print edition: 2013

ISBN: 978-1-62482-087-8

Cover design by Elderlemon Design
Layout design by Ross Burck – rossburck@gmail.com

Published in the United States of America
StoneGate Ink is an imprint of StoneHouse Ink

ALSO BY VINCENT ZANDRI

Permanence
The Innocent
Godchild
The Guilty
The Remains
Scream Catcher
The Concrete Pearl
Moonlight Falls (UNCUT EDITION)
Moonlight Mafia (A Dick Moonlight Short)
Moonlight Rises
Blue Moonlight
Murder by Moonlight
Full Moonlight (A Dick Moonlight Short)

For Lola, wherever you are…

MOONLIGHT SONATA

"I used to look forward to the day when I got too old to give a damn about women."

—James Crumley, The Last Good Kiss

Prologue

YOU'RE DROWNING.

The entirety of your fragile head thrust deep down into the watery business end of a white porcelain toilet inside the men's room of a Ralph's Bar in Albany. The water is cold and tastes vaguely of rust and urine as it enters into your mouth. You're on your knees, hands pressed flat against a piss-stained floor, the cold hard steel of a pistol barrel pressed against your spine, a bear claw of a hand shoving your head down deeper into the toilet with each thrust.

"Who sent thee?" the poet barks.

Pulling you back out by the collar on your black leather coat, you spit out the rancid water and make a desperate attempt to inhale a dose of men's room-fresh air. You want to be cooperative, being that this man is your client, whether he knows it or not. You want to at least try to answer his query. But instead you're choking, gagging, and vomiting rancid toilet water.

"Who sent thee, scoundrel?"

The pistol barrel is jammed so tight against your spine you feel like it's about to burst through skin and bone and enter into your stomach. You hear a fist banging on the men's room door. Somebody shouting to open up. Somebody who's got to drop "a big fucking deuce." But the poet doesn't care. He's locked the door. Dead-bolted it secure. He's already shot one man already, or so legend has it. What difference does it make if he shoots you too? The poet is desperate. He's on the run. He's drunk and wired up on cocaine. Enough Bolivian marching powder to fire up a power line.

You hear the barrel being cocked. You feel the mechanical action of the pistol against your spine. In a second or two, you'll hear the blast and you'll see your bullet-shredded pink stomach lining spatter up against the toilet and the graffiti-covered plaster wall—the work-in-progress canvass for the drunk and the damned.

"One more time. Who sent thee?"

You open your mouth once more, try to spit out the words. It's like tearing the skin away from the back of your throat. But in the end, you manage to form a single word.

"Agent," you whisper. Then, "Your. Fucking. Agent."

"Liar," the poet shouts, thrusting your head back into the toilet, but immediately pulling it back out, your face and head dripping wet like an overused toilet brush. "You are nothing but a scoundrel and a liar and I will have my revenge upon thee."

The pistol barrel shifts from your spine upwards to the back of your skull. In your brain, you picture the poet. His thick, white, Ernest Hemingway *Old Man and the Sea* beard, his full head of salt and pepper hair. You see his short, bull-dog build, and his many-times-broken pug nose. You see his ratty khaki safari jacket, its pockets jammed with notebooks, scraps of paper with story-lines and poems written on them, pens, pencils, unsmoked joints, cash, candy bars, and who knows what the hell else. The poet is years older than you, but bears the strength, power, and build of a rhino. A drunk, coked-up Rhino.

"No wait!" you spit. "Wait. Please. Fucking wait, Mr. Walls. I can explain."

More pounding on the door. More words. Someone about to crap his pants if you don't open up.

"My agent might be a heartless, soulless cunt who would sell out her own aging mother to make a ten-spot," Walls speaks in his deep, throaty, formal poetry reading voice. "After all, that's why I've signed on with her. But she would never stoop so low by sending a private detective in search of me. You sir, are a liar and a scoundrel."

"You don't know me."

A slap upside your head with Walls's bear claw hand. It makes your head ring.

"Cease thy banter, rogue."

The pistol is pressed harder against your skull. Now you see brain matter, blood, and bits of bone spattered against the wall. With any luck it will cover up the hand-scribbled erect cock and the phone number written below it beside with the words, *"I give great head. Call me."*

More pounding on the door. More shouts.

"She cares about you, Mr. Walls," you spit. "She needs you back at your writing desk. You're all she's got. She needs you. You need you. You need to be writing. It's my job to bring you back home."

Silence fills the bathroom, like the pause after a carefully recited stanza at a college sponsored literary reading.

"Liar," the bearded poet whispers, "turn to me."

You don't turn to him so much as he forces you up by your coat collar. Forces you up enough for you to shift from your knees to your ass.

"Open up," Walls spits. "Take thee into your mouth."

You open your mouth, your eyes shifting from the black barrel to the poet's round, bearded face. You feel the barrel slide inside, it's cold metal pressed against your tongue and against the roof of your mouth.

"Swallow until you see the colors of the noon," recites the poet from one of his most famous works. "Swallow until you lose your mind and your soul. Swallow for love. Swallow for me. Swallow your death."

You close your eyes, and wait for the barrel to come down and for the world to turn black. You've died before, so why should this time be any different? We all owe God a life. That's what Shakespeare said. And you, Richard Moonlight, part-time private eye, part-time dad of one, part-time lover, part-time scribbler of words, full-time head-case . . . You are long overdue.

But the hammer doesn't come down. That's when something else happens instead.

The pistol barrel slides back out of your mouth as the poet rises up, filling the stall with his four-by-four body. He doesn't shoot you, but he doesn't leave you in peace either.

"This is where me and thee take our leave," recites the poet. "One from the other."

When he raises up the pistol barrel, you know what's coming. You close your eyes and wait for the collision of steel against bone.

"Be advised, Mr. Moonlight, that Roger Walls will never see the inside of a prison cell again. Do we have an understanding?"

"Duly noted," you utter through clenched teeth. "But you haven't done anything wrong."

The high pitched sound of your own scared-like-a-girl voice is the last thing you remember before the men's room turns black.

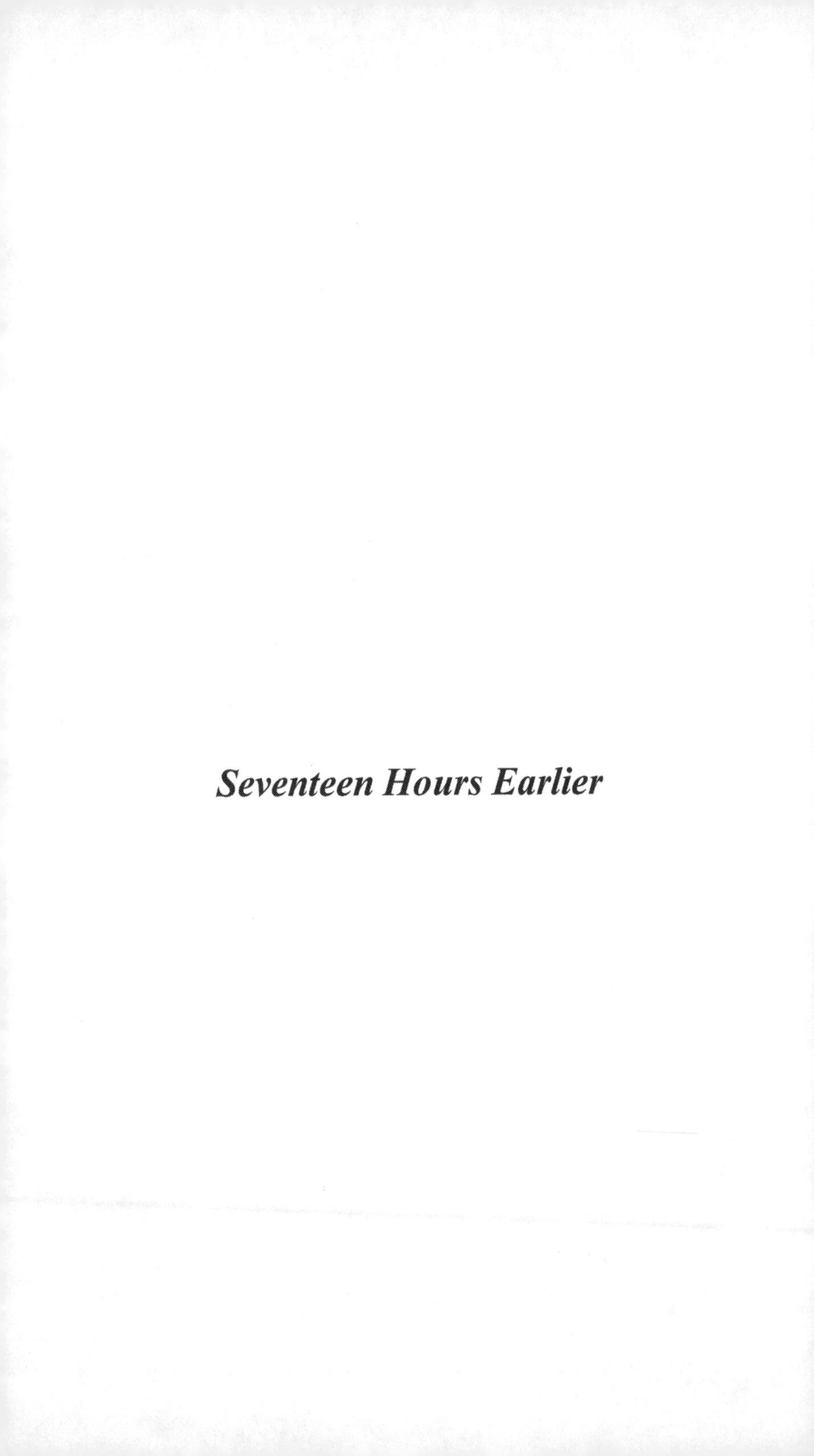

Seventeen Hours Earlier

Chapter 1

IN THE DREAM, I'M RUNNING.

Running along the side of the road. Running slow. Jogging. A nice, slow, steady gate, the blood pumping through my veins, heartbeat elevated, breathing nice even breaths in and out, a small sheen of sweat building up on my skin, coating it like a transparent glaze.

I'm feeling good. Feeling at one with my body and the fresh air. Feeling healthy. Like the little piece of bullet lodged inside my brain doesn't exist at all. Like I have nothing to look forward to but a long back-nine of a life without the threat of dying at any moment should that little fragment of bullet decide to make like an active fault line and shift.

Then the cars start passing by.

I'm facing traffic as I run along the roadside, so I can easily see the faces of the drivers and the passengers as they motor pass. There's something about the way they're gazing upon me. The drivers are slowing down and craning their necks in order to get a good look at me. They're risking injury to life and limb by taking their eyes off the road to get a full eye-fill of me, your average, everyday jogger taking in his morning run in the sun.

Or am I?

When a carload of college-age girls goes by and they begin to scream and hoot, the driver blaring the horn and swaying into the opposite lane of oncoming traffic, I know something must be up.

That's when I begin to feel a breeze.

It's slight at first. But it's a breeze alright, and it's blowing against my midsection. The farther I run away from home, the more intense the cold wind blowing against my junk becomes. I stop running. I look down at myself. It's then I realize I've left my home without my shorts on. I'm jogging along the soft shoulder of a public street in the middle of a bright busy morning, with only a t-shirt and sneakers on, the rest of me exposed to the world.

Panic fills me.

I about-face and try to sprint back to my loft. But my feet won't move. I'm paralyzed on the street-side as the cars and trucks begin piling up. They're not flying past now, satisfied with a simple rubbernecking gaze. They're pulling off to the side of the road and getting out. Old people, young people, men and women, girls and boys, cops, firemen, construction workers, students, suits, priests, bearded rabbis, you name it . . . they're all stopping their vehicles and getting out. They're standing in the road gawking at me with these wide as hell eyes, looking me up and down, feeding upon my nakedness. Upon my exposed manhood.

Those eyes . . .

. . . They are the same kind of wanting eyes that stare at me now.

Steely blue eyes that belong to a small but spunky forty-something woman by the name of Suzanne Bonchance, but who is better known in literary circles as the "Iron Lady" due to a pair of brass knuckles she keeps conspicuously perched on the edge of her desk. The same brass knuckles I can plainly see as I sit down in a black leather chair that's positioned directly before the desk. A desk so long and wide it can accommodate a dozen or more manuscripts and still leave room for the Iron Lady's many framed photos which are positioned so that a visitor like me can get a good look at them. Pics of her seated in a café in Paris with Salmon Rushdie. Pics of her dirty dancing with Jackie Collins. Pics of her walking the red carpet at the Oscars, Brad and Angelia only a few steps behind her. Pics of her standing beside Michelle and Barack Obama, a massive American flag perched on the wall behind them.

I slip my leather briefcase off my lap, set it down on the floor, and once more eye those brass knuckles.

"You ever use those before?" I ask, nodding in the direction of the steel and very illegal street fighting weapon, as she seats herself down gently into her leather swivel chair, her neck-length black hair settling perfectly upon perfectly carved shoulders. This morning those perfect shoulders are covered by a perfectly tailored gray top that perfectly matches a gray mini skirt and knee length leather boots for footwear. The forty-something woman looks like the offspring of an in-her-prime Sophia Loren and a *Friends*-era Jennifer Anniston—that is if they were ever able to physically hook up and spit out a love child. Her perfect wardrobe du jour costs more than my entire closet of Levis jeans and crew neck, all-cotton t-shirts. But then, I'm not a hotshot literary agent.

"Would you like to see me in them?" she asks, a hint of a perfect white smile forming on her red lip-sticked mouth.

"And only in them," I say. Moonlight the cagey. Or is it Moonlight the dog?

She exhales and does that positively-taken-aback eye blinking thing that all classy women do when I surprise them with my wit and charm.

"I've been warned about your humor," she says, after a calm and collecting inhale and exhale. "And about your . . ." Making like a pistol, she points an extended index finger in the direction of her right temple.

"It's okay, you can say it. You being the perfect literary agent and all."

"Suicide," she says, the word coming out with a noticeable hint of English on it. As if this New York born and bred woman were from London.

"Botched suicide, to be perfectly honest. I couldn't go through with it in the end. Call me a wimp."

"But you bear the scars. Emotional and physical." It's a statement posed like a question.

"There's a small piece of .22 caliber hollow-point lodged beside my cerebral cortex. On occasion it can cause me to pass out, especially during periods of great stress. Or it can mess with my decision making process. It can also cause me to die right now in this chair if it suddenly decides to shift. It's a hell of a way to live actually, knowing you can die at any second. Makes you appreciate the time you have all the more."

"Sounds positively warm and fuzzy," she says, the corners of her pretty little mouth perking up. "But I trust the little piece of bullet doesn't impede your performance?"

I smile.

"My performance is impeccable." It's a lie. But what the hell?

Her once cautious smile now turns into an all out ear-to-ear smile. Sitting back in her chair, she sets both hands onto the armrests. It causes her jacket to open up revealing a tight-fitting black silk blouse that's unbuttoned enough to reveal some serious cleavage and a black lace push-up bra. *Victoria Secret.*

"I'm not interested in that kind of performance," she explains.

"I'm interested in the performance of Dick Moonlight, private detective."

"I like the way you say it."

"Say what?"

"Dick."

We sit in silence while I watch the lids on her eyes rapidly rise and fall. What for some might be an uncomfortable silence, but for me is a whole-lot-of-fun kind of silence. Moonlight the ball buster.

"Why don't we get right to the heart of the matter, shall we?" the agent says after a beat.

"Goody," I say, crossing my right booted foot over my blue-jeaned knee. "Let's have it, Iron Lady."

She shifts her gaze from me to the window wall on her left, as if looking out onto the Hudson Valley helps her think.

"Are you familiar with the poet and novelist, Roger Walls?"

I steal a silent second or two to think about it. But truth be told, I don't have to think about it at all. I'm familiar with Roger Walls all right. He visited my college during my senior year back in the early ′80s when I was about to earn my BA in English Lit. Back when I'd made the solemn vow to never enter into my dad's funeral business and instead become a world-class author. Like Hemingway. Mailer. Or Walls.

Roger fucking Walls.

Sitting in front of the perfectly presented Suzanne Bonchance, I pictured the less than perfectly dressed poet/novelist donning a ratty safari jacket over a pair of worn Levis and Tony Lama cowboy boots. He wasn't very tall, but barrel-chested and he sported a black beard and black hair that by now would probably be grey. Or so I imagined. He was a bad boy writer, drunk when he arrived at the college for his reading and even drunker when he carried a bottle of Jack with him to the podium. A daring move that caused the rather conservative Providence College audience of stiff upper class profs to pucker their assholes while the English students jumped up on their feet and issued a rousing standing ovation.

"*Knives, Guns, and Bitches. Slasher Babe. The Killer Inside Her,*" I recite, recalling just a few of Walls's books. "Walls has a way with women and he reflects it in his titles."

"Roger is old school, Mr. Moonlight," Bonchance goes on, her eyes still staring out the window, no doubt onto an image of her stocky, liquor-soaked client. "He comes from a time when male writers felt they had to live by the Hemingway code. Tough, burly womanizers and drinkers. Men who lived by their word and were willing to back it up with their fists and tire irons if need be. " She sighs sadly, her eyes still glued to the great beyond. Gives me the feeling she misses the Roger Walls kind of bad boy writer. "Nowadays," she goes on, her voice more sullen, "you're lucky if a male writer takes real sugar with his double mocha Frappuccino. In today's manhood-castrated world, being a bad boy means having to give back the Oprah award or a book called *The Corrections* is about as far away from a hard-core prison novel as Justin Bieber is from Sid Vicious."

"Word up is that Walls has got an evil temper. That he shot someone once."

Her head springs back around, her eyes once more locked onto me. She's also smiling again like she's turned on by the fact that Walls is not only the last of his macho kind, but also a homicidal maniac.

"It's the truth." She nods. "He did shoot a man who encroached on his property out in Chatham near the very rural Massachusetts border. Almost thirty years ago now. Probably around the time he visited your college. He's always maintained that the man encroaching was threatening his life with a hunting rifle. Of course, he only bears a slight recollection of the event."

"Let me guess," I say. "He was inebriated at the time."

"And flying high on windowpane LSD. In any event, the man he shot did not press charges in the end."

"After being shot?"

"It was only flesh wound, Mr. Moonlight. The man with the hunting rifle was clearly in the wrong by trespassing on private property."

"Please call me Moonlight. Or, if you prefer, Ms. Bonchance, Dick."

She looks at me with an iron face. Matches her iron fist.

"Moonlight it will be," she says. "Rather poetic, I might add. An author's name if ever I heard one. Have you ever considered writing something, Moonlight? Your memoirs perhaps? I could find you a ghostwriter."

"How interesting you should suggest that," I say, reaching down with my right hand, setting it on my briefcase. "But before we get to that, what is it you would like me to do for Mr. Walls?"

"I'd like you to find him for me."

"He go missing?"

"Not officially."

"As in the cops aren't looking him." It's a question.

"The police have not been notified and nor will they be. Roger is no longer on probation for that shooting all those years ago, but his file is still open and it would be messy and complicated for him if they were to get involved."

"I understand," I say. "But how long has he been gone?"

"About a week. He's on one of his . . . how shall I say it . . ." Tossing up her hands.

"Benders," I say for her.

"Yes, benders," she repeats, dropping her hands into her lap.

"Like I said, Mr. Walls is one of the last of the bad boy writers."

"He still call Chatham home?"

"Aren't you going to write down some notes?"

I tap what's left of the little dime-sized scar on the side of my head with my index finger.

"My brain might be fragile, but it's still as sharp as the razor's edge."

"Yes, he still maintains a home there. And an apartment in Florence, Italy. He also keeps a trailer in the Baja. An Airstream actually." Then shaking her head. "Forgive me. I believe he's since sold the Baja property to a famous jazz musician."

She says Airstream with so much happy, dreamy, sexy recollection in her voice I'm surprised she doesn't faint on the spot. Tells me she's no stranger to the inside of that desert Airstream.

"How wonderful for him," I say. "Has the bad boy written anything as of late?"

She winces. Noticeably— like I picked up those brass knuckles and tossed them into her gut. Or lack thereof.

"Funny you should ask that, Moonlight," she says.

"How funny, Ms. Bonchance?"

"Please call me, Suzanne," she says. "And it's been quite a while since Mr. Walls produced a full-length novel. Ten years to be precise."

"Since *Slasher*," I say. "That book rocked. Especially the girl-on-girl threesome scenes. Lots of violence too."

"Yes, you would be his kind of audience, I dare say, Moonlight. The movie did quite well too."

"Brad Pitt. How can it not do well? Walls must have made a fortune."

"Indeed. Problem is, that kind of money doesn't last. Not when you possess the rather expensive habits of our Mr. Walls. One of which is divorce. He's created a hobby out of it. You can't imagine the child support and alimony payments he must make on a monthly basis alone."

"Or that he is supposed to make anyway."

"Correct, Moonlight. All too often he, um, let's say, forgets to write out his checks."

"Another good reason for keeping the cops out of this."

"Hmm, yah think?"

I smile.

She smiles.

"So then, Ms. Bonchance, bottom line here."

"Bottom line, Moonlight? A working Roger Walls is a money-making Roger Walls. He's also a sober Roger Walls and a responsible bill-paying Roger Walls."

"I see. It means you can keep up with the payments on your Porsche and your house in The Hamptons."

"How did you know I have a house in The Hamptons?"

"Lucky guess." Moonlight the intuitive. Then, "Any idea where I might start looking for him? He got a favorite local bar?"

"Lots of favorites. So I assume."

"Can you recall a specific one?"

She shakes her head.

"I never frequented those kinds of places with him. We engaged in more civilized behavior. Like dinner at the 677 Prime Steak House in downtown Albany." Laughing. What a writer might describe as *sardonically*. "Correction. I ate, and he drank."

"Maybe there's a joint in Chatham I can check out. Not a big town."

"Excellent, Moonlight. I can already see what a master detective you are."

"Hey, you hired me. Warts and all. He have any family?"

"Parents are dead. He's got a sister somewhere. But not in New York. Don't know whether she's older or younger or even still alive for that matter."

"His ex-wives live around here?"

Shaking her head. "His present wife still resides in the Albany area. Look Walls up on Wikipedia. You'll find his list of love interests there. The newest one's an actress. Got lucky with some minor parts in some Showtime stuff. A sprinkling of television commercials. Hot little piece of eye candy, you ask me."

"And Walls has a major sweet tooth, I take it. What's her name?"

"Sissy. Young thing. Bit of a partier. Has driven Roger to the edge more than once."

"She mind if I pay her a visit?"

"I'm not sure her minding is important."

"Gotcha. Anyone else you know I should check with? Friends? Drinking buddies?"

"Roger doesn't believe in friends. 'No friends, no enemas' he often preaches." Then raising her right hand like a brilliant thought has just flashed inside her head. "There is one man you might try. His name is Gregor Oatczuk. A writing professor at the university MFA program."

"Sounds important. But that name. Sounds like *Upchuck*." I make a face, like I feel like puking.

"He's as close to a friend as Roger has around here, even though Roger thinks of him as a bore. And yup, hell of name to be born with. He should change it."

"You got a number for him?"

She leans up in her chair, picks up her phone. "I'll call his office. Tell him you'll be coming."

She dials and I wait. When someone answers she asks for

this Oatczuk character by name. When she's told he isn't in, she explains the situation to the person who must be his secretary. Then she hangs up.

"He'll call me back. When he does, I'll send him your way."

"Thanks."

"Find the writer for me. And I will pay you handsomely. Plus all expenses and a nice fat bonus."

"With real money?"

"And then some."

"Goodie. I might ask you to pay me in another way as well." Once more, I set my hand back down on my brief case.

Her eyes go wide, giving me that same up-and-down look they gave me when I first walked in.

"Excuse me, Moonlight?"

"Not that kind of payment, Ms. Bonchance," I say, pulling the briefcase up and onto my lap. "But I have a small confession to make. A moment ago you asked me if I've ever written anything. Well, here's your answer." Opening up the flap on the leather case, I slide out the manuscript. "It's a sort of fictional memoir. A detective story."

Silence fills the office. A thick weighted silence that makes my chest go tight.

"My list is quite full, Moonlight. I was only joking before when I suggested you write your memoirs. Truth is, I'm not really taking on new projects. It's one of the reasons I moved my office up to sleepy little Albany. I no longer have to compete in the Manhattan rat race."

I stand, the now empty case in one hand, the manuscript in the other.

"Just read a few pages," I say. "If you don't like it, no harm done. Consider it a personal favor. I'll be on the case of your missing writer regardless."

She cocks her head, sits up straight, feet flat on the floor.

"Ok, leave it," she says.

I set the manuscript onto the table. It takes me by surprise when she practically dives across the desk to snatch it up. A hungry fish on a fat, juicy worm. Sitting back in her chair, she reads the cover page.

"*Moonlight Falls*," she says, with a sly grin. "Not bad, Moonlight. Not a bad title if I say so myself. Maybe you will have something here after all." Setting the book back down on the table, she stands and comes around her desk.

"I can stay while you read it," I say, reaching out, setting my open hand on her perfect shoulder, giving it a slight squeeze. Moonlight the charming.

"Not today, thank you," she says. "I'll start on it tonight in bed."

"That's a very nice thought."

"I'm sure it is. In the mean time you have work to do."

I start for the door, but stop almost before I get a couple of steps.

"Oh, before I forget," I say, turning back around. "Do you have a book with a recent picture of Walls on it?"

She shakes her head, annoyed. Like she wants me to leave already.

"I just moved my office up from the city. The books don't arrive until later in the week. Google him, or just stop at a bookstore on the way back to your office."

"They still have bookstores?"

"Yes, you can still find one or two in existence. The State University Barnes & Noble on Washington Avenue just down the road from the campus is the best one these days. Roger will have signed editions there and, if you head there now, it's possible Oatczuk will call me back and you can kill two birds with one stone."

I stand there. Silent.

"Is there something else, Moonlight?"

"My fee."

"Whatever it is, I'll pay it."

"Buck fifty per day plus expenses."

"Give your billing address to my secretary out front," she says. But then she quickly throws up her hands. "Oh crap, my secretary is off today. We can take care of your billing needs tomorrow. In any case, call me right away when you have some news on Roger. Day or night."

"Day or night?" I say opening the door. "I wouldn't want to wake Mr. Bonchance."

She laughs.

"I think, Moonlight," she says. "Therefore I'm single."

"I'm a private dick, Ms. Bonchance," I say. "Therefore I'm divorced."

Chapter 2

HERE'S THE DEAL: I'M going to die.

Okay, I know what you're thinking: We're all gonna die one day. But that's not what I'm talking about here. This isn't about the great, cosmic, circle-of-life-Elton-John-Walt-Disney-soundtrack kind of spiel. What I'm trying to tell you is that it's very possible, if not highly likely, that I can die right now in the middle of making this sentence.

No lie.

No fabrication.

No drama for drama's sake.

The truth: There's a little piece of .22 caliber hollow-point bullet lodged snug up against my cerebral cortex. If it should suddenly shift for any one of a thousand good reasons (the least of which being that it simply wants to), it can render me instantly paralyzed, comatose, and ultimately dead.

I'm not the type of guy a life insurance salesman likes to call first thing on a Monday morning. I'm not the kind of discerning shopper who can buy now, pay later at zero percent interest. A banker would laugh at the prospect of extending me a thirty-year mortgage much less a thirty-day note. You just can't bank on the fact that at the end of the day, Richard "Dick" Moonlight, Captain Head-Case, is still gonna be around to pay up.

I live my life according to the death that shadows me so closely I can feel its cold darkness like a constant icy breeze blowing against my spine. Death might be a pale rider, but it's also a constant companion. We've grown to know one another so well that we've become friends, almost. Me, the living Dick Moonlight, and the very soon-to-be dead Dick Moonlight. We're one big happy family. We should trade recipes.

Living with death has taught me something. It's taught me that when I am finally gone, I want to leave something for my ten-year-old son, Bear. I want to leave a record of my life so he will know his real dad. We don't get to see one another all the time since he lives in California with his mom, my ex-wife Lynn. But that doesn't mean we are ever far from one another's thoughts. And maybe Bear believes I will always be around for him. But I know that the opposite is far more likely. He will never know the real me should that bullet happen to change position and my world suddenly goes black—the skin, flesh and blood, all too cold.

But there's some good news in all of this. A silver lining as it were. The uncertainty over my longevity, or lack thereof, recently brought me to one solid conclusion: I want to make a record of my life. All forty-eight years of it. And not one of those sappy home-spun videos like they dramatize in all those Lifetime-channel-cancer-victim movies. You know, the one where the former A-list-now-turned-B-list actor gets liver cancer just in time for his kid's third birthday, and since he won't live to see the fourth, he decides to make a series of advice videos the kid can enjoy for years and years long after the old man is worm food. That's not for me, and my bushy-haired kid would probably be freaked out at the idea of having his dead dad in his face all the time.

Instead I want to write my memoirs.

But I'm not writer, right?

Truth revealed, I not only possess an English Lit degree, I had every intention of becoming a novelist upon graduation. But somehow life got in the way and I became a cop. Money, love, marriage, the birth of a child, and eventually, divorce, all had something to do with putting off the dream for more than twenty years. But now that I'm not a cop and only a part-time private dick, there's really no excuse for not putting pen to paper. Which is how I came to write *Moonlight Falls*. The first book about my fall from grace at the Albany Police Department and from my marriage to Lynn. It also details my love affair with the lovely Scarlett Montana, the wife of my former department boss, and an illegal body parts harvesting operation we all got mixed up in along with a highly lethal crew of Russian mobsters. It's not a happy memoir or a feel-good-boy-gets-the-girl at the end, thriller. It's more like a train wreck, watch-the-girl-walk-out-on-me-yet-again life story. But it's an honest story nonetheless.

There's more to the book than I'm letting on about right now, but far be it from me to be a spoiler. For all I know, the perfect Iron Lady lit agent herself, Suzanne Bonchance, might hate it. If that happens I'll pretty much forget about being a published author. But I'll still continue to write the memoirs for as long as I live, be it one hour, one more day, or ten more years. And they will be meant for one set of eyes, and one set of eyes only. Those deep brown eyes that belong to my son, Bear.

Driving.

In the direction of pretty much the only bookstore left alive in Albany since the outbreak of e-Books. The State University Barnes

& Noble booksellers. Maybe a bookstore is the last place I should start looking for a writer like Walls. Maybe I should simply start searching every bar in the State of New York or, at the very least, the bars that grace the little town of Chatham out in the country. But that would be like searching for a needle in a stack of needles and if Walls is hanging out in a small-town bar he won't exactly be missing in action will he? It's been a while since I read anything penned by Roger Walls. I figure if I'm going to try and find him, maybe it'd be a good idea to at least grab his most current book of fiction or maybe poetry and get inside his head a little.

As advertised, the chain bookstore is located not far down the road from the main entrance to the Albany State campus. To my surprise, the lot is packed. But I manage to squeeze Dad's pride-and-joy black funeral hearse in between a brand new pickup truck and a beater from another era that most likely belongs to a high school or college student. It always makes me nervous having to sandwich Dad's ride in between two other vehicles. I know the dangers of door dings and fender benders. Doesn't matter that he's long dead, in every physical sense of the word. That Dad is looking down upon me, keeping tabs on how I maintain his ride, there is no doubt. That he still distrusts me, there is also no doubt.

Who says books are dead?

The Barnes & Noble is bustling with activity when I enter into its cavernous spaces. There're lots of people browsing the half dozen tables strategically set up in front of the doors as you walk in. The tables that carry the brand new thirty-dollar hard-cover releases by the same five or six mystery authors the *New York Times* keeps at the top of their lists perpetually. While a dozen or so people are staring down at the books, no one seems to be buying them. Why buy a thirty-dollar hard-cover when you can get it for pocket change on your e-reader?

I head into the depths of the store until I come to the tall bookcase that houses the poetry section. I head all the way to the W's when I spot a young woman standing up against the far wall, a book gripped in her left hand, her eyes glued to its pages.

"Pardon me," I say, trying to get a look at the title that has her so engrossed. When it turns out to be a Roger Walls book, I know it's my lucky day. I decide to beam some Moonlight charm. "Roger Walls, huh? I'm a big fan too."

She raises up her head, tosses me a smile that's filled with perfect white teeth surrounded by a healthy tan face, deep-set brown eyes, and a forehead too young and optimistic to be marred with wrinkles, all stunningly veiled in thick, light brown hair parted delicately on the left side.

"How nice for you?" she whispers, as if we're in a library.

"I've read all his novels," I say. "But not his poetry."

She nods, lowers her book so that its spine brushes up against the portion of bare thigh that's exposed between the hem of her cotton skirt and her black leather, knee-high boots.

"I'm an MFA student at Albany State," she explains, shifting the thick strap on her canvass shoulder bag.

"How nice for you too. What discipline?"

"Writing. In this case, poetry."

"Lots of jobs out there for poets these days. You should do well." Moonlight the witty.

She shoots me this wide-eyed look like I'm crazy. But nice crazy.

"I'm not concerned with getting a job. I'm going to be a writer. A poet and a novelist."

"How stupid of me. I was groomed for the funeral business a long, long time ago. Which is why I became a cop."

"You're a cop?"

"Used to be. Now I'm a private detective, and I'm also trying my hand at some writing too."

She nods, pursing thick red lips.

"I imagine that by the time one gets to be your age, one must have lots of stories one wants to tell."

"With age comes wisdom. But I'm not that old, nor wise."

She flashes me a Pearl Drops toothpaste grin. "You remind me of my dad."

"Your dad's cool and hot, huh?"

She laughs, slaps her young thigh with that book.

"I don't know you, Mister."

I hold out my hand. "My dad raised me better than that. Moonlight is the name. Life and death is the game."

She reaches out tentatively with her free hand, takes hold of mine, gives it a weak shake.

"Erica Beckett," she says, her tan face now beaming red with embarrassment. "That's Beckett like Samuel Beckett. He's a distant relative."

"Nice meeting you Erica the poet who's related to Samuel Beckett. How the hell can you miss with a name and history like that?"

"That's what I say, Mr. Moonlight."

"So, back to my original question: Why the interest in Roger Walls?"

She steals back her hand.

"My prof is a big Walls nut. Claims to be best friends with him actually. I'm not sure I believe him. Walls is, like, super famous. And my prof is just . . . well, my prof."

"He's not a writer?"

"Well, he is a writer. He's even published. But he's not famous like Roger Walls and let's face it, writers who teach are writers who don't make money or they wouldn't be teaching." Another roll of those big brown, reflective pools. "God, sometimes I think he's in love with Roger. Or wants to be him anyway."

"Wouldn't you?"

Another wide-eyed look that screams: "Huh?"

"I mean, if you were a guy. A guy poet. Like your Uncle Samuel."

She laughs again, brushing back her smooth hair with her free hand. Not nervously but confidently.

"Oh, I get you now. Yeah, sure, I guess. It would be fun to be rich and famous just for making shit up. And be able to travel all the time, and party like a wild animal."

"Don't forget all that sex."

"Oh, yes," she bellows. I can practically smell the excitement and hormones just oozing off her twenty-something body. "The sex must rock."

"What's you prof's name?"

"Um . . . Oatczuk. . . And no I'm not making that up."

"Oatczuk. Well, coincidence of coincidences, my client wants me to talk with him. Thinks he might have an idea of Roger's whereabouts."

"Well, isn't this your lucky day. I'm his secretary as a part of my work-study program. I'm the one who spoke with Suzanne Bonchance just a little while ago."

"SmAlbany," I say. "Three degrees of separation. Not six."

"Isn't that the truth. Serendipity is easier around these parts."

We stand silent for a moment while I quickly browse a few of the Walls's poetry titles. *Sex and Slander . . . Cock and Bull . . . Pink . . . .* I grab a copy of *Pink,* open up to the title page, observe the copyright date. It's this year. Maybe Walls hasn't been writing novels lately, but that doesn't mean he's been resting on his literary laurels. 'Course, even I know that nobody makes money from poetry. I arbitrarily flip the pages to one of the poems located in the middle of the volume. It's called "Solitary Confinement."

Both hands bloody from the brutal work of murder
A blade with a jagged edge
A fully erect cock
A man stands all alone in the desert
Man severs his testicles
Bloody separation
Beautiful freedom

Quintessential Roger Walls. Angry, violent, take no prisoners. Not exactly bedtime reading for the kids either.

Closing the book, I turn it over and gaze down at an author photo that I can only assume is recent. Walls, with a full head of wavy salt and pepper hair and a thick beard to match. He's looking directly into the camera with the dark eyes of a hungry wildebeest, and the scowl painted on his face doesn't make it look like he's politely inviting you to check out his poetry, but fucking daring you. Dressed in a black t-shirt under his usual ratty safari jacket I can practically smell the cigarette smoke oozing out his nostrils, the whiskey on his breath, and the pussy on his fingers.

And then a light bulb flashes on over my head. I reach into my pocket, pull out a business card.

"Erica, will you be seeing your professor anytime soon? The one who's good buddies with Walls?"

She takes the card in her hand, glances down at it for a few moments.

"Never met a real private eye before," she says. "Only seen one on TV. And in books."

"You don't lower yourself to reading detective novels, do you Erica Beckett, candidate for an MFA in writing?"

She looks over one shoulder and then the other, as if we're surrounded by her fellow students and profs and not just books.

"Can you keep a secret, Mr. Moonlight?"

"Is the dead pope Polish?"

"I absolutely love mysteries. I gobble them up. I'm going to write one someday. Along with my poetry."

A second light going off.

"I just finished my first, myself. It's based on one of my first cases. It's called *Moonlight Falls*. I have an agent interested." Okay, I'm stretching it a bit. "But I'd love it if you ever wanted to take a look and give me your opinion."

She smiles, genuinely.

"Sure. You have another one of those cards?"

I hand her one. She pulls a pen from her bag and writes down her email, hands it back to me. I glance at it and pocket it.

"Just email it to me. I'm happy to take a break from all this academic bullshit."

"Happy to help a future Amazon bestseller. Say, do you think you can arrange a little come-to-Jesus between me and Oat . . . um . . . whatever his last name is?"

"It's Gregor Oatczuk. O-A-T, like Quaker Oats. Without the 's' and with a 'czuk' tagged onto the end of it. Like woodchuck, only spelled differently. In this case, C-Z-U-K."

"I'd like to talk with him."

"Do you mind my asking what about?"

"Our old boy Roger has gone missing and his agent has hired me to go find him and cart him back home to his writing desk so that he can make her some money. Or something like that. Word on the literary street is that he hasn't penned a new novel in ten years.

Or published one anyway."

"Oh my, Mr. Moonlight. How positively interesting. Can I be of any help? Like I said, I love a good mystery."

"You can start by helping me set up a meeting with Gregor Oatczuk. The sooner, the better. Maybe even today."

"I'll get in touch with him as soon as I leave here and email you right away."

I hold out my hand once more. She takes it and shakes it harder this time.

"Erica Beckett, grand niece of the great Samuel Beckett, you are hereby deputized in the name of the father and the son and Richard 'Dick' Moonlight."

"Great. I'm your girl."

"If only it were true," I say, shelving the book of poetry, about facing and starting toward the center of the store.

"Oh, Mr. Moonlight," Erica calls out.

I stop, turn back in her direction.

"What is it?"

"What's the name of your book, again?"

"*Moonlight Falls*."

"And the detective in the story is you? Dick Moonlight?"

"Yup, it's a story about a private dick."

"I bet it's a very *long* story," she says, shooting me a wink.

Couldn't have said it better myself.

Chapter 3

DRIVING BACK TOWARD THE center of the city in the funeral hearse, I pull off the road and park in a 7–Eleven parking lot, dial Suzanne Bonchance from the cell. Since I'm calling her private mobile number, she picks up after only a couple of ringy-dingys.

"I'm already working my first lead," I tell her after she answers with a simple yet direct, and very French, I might add, "Bonchance!"

"It's not necessary for you to call me every time you make some progress, Mr. Moonlight."

"I'm sorry. Thought you might like to know."

"Agents never . . . and I repeat . . . *never* like to be called. We do all the calling. Not the other way around."

"Don't you want to know?"

"Know what?"

"About my lead?"

"Okay, what is it?"

"I just happened to run into a very attractive young lady at the Barnes & Noble who is, at present, an MFA student at the state university and Upchuck's private secretary. She also just happened to be cruising through some of Roger Walls's poetry titles. In fact, she's the woman you spoke to when you called Oatczuk's office earlier."

"Oatczuk. And yes, thank goodness for serendipity. And is this going to be a long story?"

"Yes, thank goodness for serendipity. That's what I said. Because it also so happens that Oatczuk just might have some idea of where we can locate our wandering writer."

"No shit, Moonlight!" she barks. "We've been over this already, which is why I made the phone call to his office in the first place."

"Just doing my job, good Luck."

"Excuse me, Moonlight?"

"Your last name. Bonchance . . . it means 'good luck' in French. Get it?"

"Yes, it's my name. And I prefer the French spelling and pronunciation."

I picture the sharply dressed brunette agent seated in her black swivel chair, rolling her eyes, while checking the cuticles on her full-masted fingers for any imperfections in the weekly manicure. A crack, a chip, a smudge.

"Well my guess is if there's anyone who knows where Walls ran off to," I say, "it will probably be him."

Silence. Heavy, foreboding, oozing through the connection like mustard gas.

"Moonlight, I'm fully aware of your reputation as a ladies' man. Promise me you won't go near the young lady in question while working for me. If something unsavory or illicit should occur, I would also be held responsible and that is simply not acceptable in my profession. I have a stable of authors and their careers to think of."

"The young lady I speak of is over seventeen and in fact over twenty one. What she does with her body is her business, especially if she can't help herself when it comes to falling under my spell. I'm sure you're already familiar with said spell."

More silence. Mustard gas laced with cyanide. I tend to have that kind of effect on women.

"Mr. Moonlight, before we go any further, I am delighted to maintain a professional relationship with you and only a professional relationship. As for Professor Oatczuk, he is most definitely not Walls's best friend. He only wishes he was."

"You know him personally?"

"Tragically, I do. He's been asking me to represent him for years. I don't go a single year without one of his train wrecks landing inside my inbox."

"Bad writing?"

"His craft is excellent. It's just that the man and his work are a positively insufferable yawn. And can you imagine me trying to sell a novel by an author named Oatczuk?"

"He can change his name. Take on a nom de plume."

"Yes, but the writer must be willing to do so. Which Oatczuk most definitely is not."

"You talked over the possibility with him then. Must be you liked something about his work."

"No, I didn't. And he's not a writer. He's a teacher. You know what they say about teaching."

"Yah," I say recalling my conversation with Erica, "he who can't do, teaches."

"Exactly," she agrees, sighing. "Now is there anything else I can do for you, Mr. Moonlight?"

My pulse picks up, just a little.

"You haven't um, started my, um . . ."

"No, Moonlight. I'm not that fast. Besides, I read at night in bed. I told you that."

"Ah yes, I remember. Books in the place of a real man."

"I don't feel I need to remind you of that again."

"Not necessary. I read you loud and clear, Good Luck. One more thing. I'm alone for dinner tonight. I was wondering if you might like to have a quiet drink and something to eat?"

"Are you asking me out on a date, Moonlight?"

"Actually, I'm seeing someone. It would be purely professional."

"Why don't I believe you?"

"About what part? The dating someone or the purely professional thing?"

"Both."

"Well, at least think about it. You might want to get to know the author if you're going to represent his book."

A laugh. Loud enough to make me pull the phone from my ear.

"Do you know how many writers who would slice off their manhood to have a shot at me being their agent?"

"Let me guess. A lot."

"Yes, a lot. More than a lot. I will let you know if I want to take you on or not."

"Okay, Good Luck, have it your way. But I can tell you one thing."

"What's that?"

"I'm not about to cut off my Johnson for you. That's where I draw the line."

"We'll see about that, Moonlight. We'll just have to see."

She hangs up.

I feel a dull pain in my midsection, as if Suzanne Bonchance, the Iron Lady of the literary industry, has just managed to emasculate me not with a blade, but with only her words. I get out of the hearse, head into the 7–Eleven for a six-pack of beer while contemplating that very disturbing notion.

Chapter 4

BY THE TIME I get back to my loft inside the abandoned Port of Albany, I've already got an email from my new friend, Erica. Standing at the island counter in the kitchen area of the riverside brick building that once housed the offices of a shipping company, I click on the email:

> *Hi again, Mr. Moonlight. I spoke to Professor Oatczuk and he said that he would have no problem if you stopped by as early as this afternoon. He had no idea Roger Walls was "missing in action," as he put it, and he wants to help. Here's my number: 555-2354 . . . Give me a call soon as you get this and we can go see him together if you like. ;)*
> *Erica*

"Go see him together," I whisper, staring at the little green, winking smiley face posted at the end of her sentence. "Me likey."

I pull my mobile from my thin black leather coat, dial the number she gave me, wait for a pick up.

"Mr. Moonlight?" she answers, instead of a generic "Hello."

"You recognize my number already?"

"I put it in my list of contacts after you slipped me your card. I'm your deputy remember?"

"How could I ever forget? Where do you want to meet?"

"Do you know how to navigate the state campus? It's just beyond the bookstore where we first met this morning."

"Where we first met. How romantic, Ms. Beckett."

She giggles. "So do you know the campus?"

"It's been a while. I used to do a little partying there with friends back in my day."

"Meet me at the front gates. Washington Avenue entrance. Two o'clock sharp."

"How will I recognize you?"

"I'll be the sexy hottie in the lipstick-red Porsche convertible."

"Expensive ride. Thought you were a writing student?"

"I'm a woman who gets what she wants, Mr. Moonlight."

"That's funny. I'm a guy who gets what he wants."

"We'll see about that, old man."

"Who you calling old?"

I'd wait for an answer. But she's already hung up.

Chapter 5

I LOOK AT MY WATCH.

Ten-fifteen on a bright Monday morning in the early spring. I've already had my coffee and it's too early for lunch and way too early for one of those cold beers that I bought. I could take Erica up on her offer of looking at my manuscript, but then my built-in shit detector tells me to back off on that notion. I once heard a well-known writer say that he never read another person's writing in progress. Why? Because if it was good, he'd hate it since it would mean more competition. But if it was bad, he'd hate it even more for wasting his time. What all this means is that I'll have to continue working. And since Bonchance is paying a buck-fifty an hour, I figure I'd better get started right away. Whether I like it or not. Moonlight the barely self-employed.

My laptop is sitting out on the island counter.

I open it up, enter in my security code, and allow it to boot up. When it's up and running, I click onto the Google homepage. In the search space, I don't type in "Roger Walls." Instead I listen to my gut and what comes out instead is, "Suzanne Bonchance."

Sure, Walls is my only concern at the moment. Or should be

my only concern. But I'm curious about Bonchance. Why would a powerful literary agent like her decide to hire a head-case like myself when she could obviously afford a much better one who doesn't have a bullet lodged inside his brain. But then, it isn't up to me to uncover her reasoning. Maybe she doesn't have a reason for hiring me other than she likes the name.

Moonlight Private Detective Services.

Kind of poetic when you think about it. Slides off the lips and tongue like nectar from the poetry Gods. The tonal opposite of Oatczuk.

I click on the enter key and observe the Suzanne Bonchance search results.

The top entry is from the William Morris Agency. Even I've heard of them. Mega agents for the world's mega bestsellers. I click onto it. Bonchance is listed as one of their top agents. The site must not be updated since I know for a fact that she is now working for herself. Working for herself up in Albany, to be precise, one hundred forty miles from the ground zero of literary fortune and glory.

I keep browsing.

There's LinkedIn and Facebook accounts, which I skip over. But then I notice an article from the *New York Observer* on Manhattan's Top Ten Agents, of whom you-guessed-it resides at the top. I click onto it, and the perfect Ms. Bonchance is standing sandwiched in between punk poet Goddess, Patti Smith and Anthony Bourdain, the travel writer/cook superstar. They're dressed to the nines and each of them are holding glasses of red wine and looking plenty drunk. But fashionably drunk. The date on the article is November 15 of last year. It's March in the new year and Bonchance seems to have left the glitz and the limelight of Manhattan for little old Albany. Doesn't make sense. Or maybe it does. She claims to have a full list. Maybe she's looking to kick back in our little sleepy backwater. Give her more time to read. In bed. Alone.

I continue with the search.

More photos of Bonchance hanging out with the rich and famous.

I decide to click on the "News" option. An article from the *New York Times* appears. It's dated December 24th. This past Christmas Eve. There's yet another photo of the attractive agent, but it's just a head shot. And she's not smiling. Instead, she's sneering at the camera, half her outstretched hand blocking the lower portion of her face, as if she were trying to block it from the paparazzi completely. I gaze at the headline.

Power Agent Pilfers Client's Story!

"Bingo!" I say aloud in the loft.

I read the article.

It describes the uber-agent of having been accused by a New York City-based writer by the name of Ian Brando of having stolen his story. According to the piece, Brando penned an urban thriller called *The Chased and The Dead*. It was about a punk rocker and his girlfriend who engage in a cross country run after a bank heist and get into a shit storm of trouble. Apparently Brando submitted the book to Bonchance, who inevitably rejected it, but then at the same time stole the story and sold it as the basis for her first personally penned screenplay which she called *Ninth Life*.

The article goes on to say that Bonchance making the jump from agent to writer was big news since that kind of thing rarely happens. Although she refused to give in to accusations of plagiarism, she did in the end agree to settle with Brando out of court for a half a million dollars in damages. From that point on, Suzanne Bonchance's reputation as the Iron Lady in NYC turned rusty. The top agent fell hard and her competitors enjoyed kicking her while she was down.

I sit back in my chair and think things over.

No wonder Bonchance is so concerned about getting Walls back. If he is, at present, her only client, she's probably desperate. Still, we have a problem now, Ms. Good Luck and me. The problem is one of trust. My dad might have been a mortician, but he taught me a thing or two about business, and one of his major rules was to always establish a trust between you and your client. Otherwise the professional relationship will always be marred by suspicion and animosity. That in mind, I pick up the phone, dial Bonchance's number.

"You aren't telling me the truth," I say when she answers.

"Who the hell is this?" she barks.

"You know who it is. I'm sure my number comes up on the caller ID."

"My assistant must be out having coffee for you to have gotten right through to me, Moonlight."

"Bullshit, Suzanne. Who you trying to kid? I thought she was out for the day? Fact is, you don't have an assistant. You can't afford one. I'm surprised you can afford the rent in that building. No wonder you hired me. I'm the cheapest PI in the city."

"You came highly recommended."

"By who? The cops? They hate me and I don't have enough satisfied clients for you to come up with a personal reference. I don't have a website either."

"Okay, you're cheap. Are you proud we've established that?"

"You stole a book, put your name on it, and sold it to Hollywood."

Bonchance exhales a sigh so profound, I feel it more than hear it.

"Tell you what, Moonlight, let's stop and reverse the direction of this conversation."

"Brakes officially applied. What is it you have in mind, Good Luck?"

"It's almost lunch time. Why don't you meet me at Prime for lunch in a half-hour? I'll come clean and then you can get on with the business of finding Roger Walls. Agreed?"

"So long as you're paying, Fancy."

"Of course I'm paying."

"Just making sure you still have room left on your Amex."

"See you in thirty, wise-ass."

She hangs up.

I go to my closet, pick out a clean shirt for my fancy lunch with my future literary agent.

Chapter 6

"THE TRUTH, MR. MOONLIGHT, is that I do not have an assistant whom I can afford. Nor a secretary to answer my phones. Nor to bring me a bagel and cappuccino every morning. But make no mistake, I do have the money to pay you."

Bonchance is speaking to me from across a small, white tablecloth-covered table at Mario's 677 Prime Steakhouse, Albany's most expensive and trendiest eatery. The type of place that serves thirty-dollar lunch entrées with cloth napkins and where you use proper words like "nor" and "whom." The management requires you to wear a tie and a jacket when lunching in their establishment, neither of which I anticipated when choosing my usual wardrobe of black leather coat over Levis, worn-in combat boots, and a blue button-down. Un-ironed. Luckily the maître d' proved to be a real Johnny-on-the-spot upon my arrival by supplying me with the necessary house tie and jacket. In the meantime, Suzanne is still dressed in the same ravishing gray skirt and matching jacket she was wearing only a few hours ago when we first met, her perfect shoulder-length hair even more perfect now that she is exposing her famous face to the general public.

"Why didn't you level with me from the beginning, Good Luck?" I say, pulling a thick jumbo shrimp from a stainless steel bowl set on the middle of the table and dipping it into a pool of spicy blood-red sauce located in the bowl's center.

"Stop calling me that," the literary agent insists, an expression of scorn painting her face. "And be careful not to get any of the sauce on your tie or they will charge me for that too."

Setting my shrimp back down, I stuff the tie into my shirt. I follow with a small sip of my Budweiser beer. I'm probably the only patron of this establishment to order a Bud. I'm surprised they even carry it. I'm definitely the only one who is drinking beer from the bottle and not a nice tall, chilled pilsner glass.

"Better?" I say.

"Much," she says, that scornful look now replaced with a fake smile. I liked the scorn look better.

"So back to my question," I say, picking the shrimp back up and drowning it in the red sauce. "Why not level with me? We need to trust one another if we're going to work together."

"I didn't feel my past was any of your business. Simple as that."

I take the shrimp in my mouth, bite down. Sweet, succulent, textural, the tang and heat of the horse radish-laced red sauce the perfect compliment. If only lunch were like this every day, instead of burgers, fries, and Diet Cokes.

I proceed to tell her what I know about her past and the book-stealing incident while finishing up my shrimp and wishing I could order another round without appearing uncouth for such a high brow establishment. Moonlight the socially conscious.

"Reports were greatly exaggerated. I would never willingly compromise my reputation for a single book or a quickie sale." Bonchance is nibbling on a toothpick-speared olive that came with her clean martini. Nibbling sexily, I might add. "I merely used the gentleman in question's title. Something I was perfectly in my right to do since titles can't be copy written."

"Then you didn't use any of the story." It's a question.

She bites the olive off the toothpick, and washes it down with a gulp of martini.

"Okay, I might have borrowed certain elements," she sighs after a beat. "Look, Moonlight. I'll level with you further. I fucked up. I used the bulk of his story for my own and in doing so exercised a serious lack of judgment. I also ostracized myself from my colleagues, my agency, and my friends. Happy?" Her eyes filling up. "I lost almost my entire list of clients, not to mention that horrible lawsuit you speak of. For a while, it looked like my career was finished."

"How many clients did you lose exactly?"

"All. Of. Them . . . Except . . ."

"He stuck with you, didn't he?"

Her wet eyes light up as she steals another sip of martini.

"Yes, Roger stayed true. God bless him."

"But he's flown the coop, and without him home, healthy and writing, you just might end up having to look for a real job."

"Something like that. Which is why I need you to be in search of him. Not here eating shrimp."

The waiter arrives with our steaks. As he sets them in front of us I breathe in the sizzling aroma of a great cut of meat cooked medium rare. Perfection. I cut into the meat, pop the piece into my mouth. It melts. I hardly have to chew. If that little piece of bullet lodged inside my brain shifts right now and I die, I will die a happy head-case.

"It's why you hired me isn't it?" I pose. "I come cheap. And you're broke."

She cuts off a piece of steak that wouldn't feed a church mouse, places it in her mouth.

"It's true, I checked up on you with the police. You don't necessarily come highly recommended Moonlight. That much is also true. But on the other hand, you weren't described as completely inept either. And yes, you are affordable."

I set my fork down, touch the scar on the side of my head. "So my former brothers and sisters in blue are the ones who revealed my past."

"Yes, they made me very aware of your botched suicide. We are not perfect, us humans."

"Much as we try," I say. And then, changing subject. "This lawsuit you were involved with. It's all over? No further trouble from the plaintiff?"

"Why are we still talking about this when it has nothing whatsoever to do with Roger? No further trouble from the plaintiff, I guess. Does that answer your query?"

I eat another bite of steak.

"Why do you say, 'I guess'? That means you *are* having trouble."

She shrugs her shoulders.

"I've gotten maybe a few prank calls."

"Would you describe those calls as threatening?"

She sets her fork and knife onto the plate rim, picks up her drink, downs what's left in one swift pull. Setting the now empty martini glass back down, she immediately gestures for the waiter to bring her another. I stare at my bottle of beer. I've barely taken a sip.

"The man who calls me tells me that one day he will get me for what I've done."

"That's what he says to you? Nothing else?"

"That's all he says."

"Is it the man who sued you?"

"I have no way of knowing."

"How can you not know, Suzanne?"

"We never went to trial. I settled for that ungodly amount, knowing the whole time the book probably never would have sold anyway."

"But you liked the story enough to steal it."

That scorned face again.

"I borrowed it. *Borrowed*. Borrowed certain elements."

"Enough for you to be sued over plagiarism."

"Yes I settled to get it over with and to cauterize the bleeding. I never met Ian Brando in the flesh. Never spoke with him. I have no idea what his voice sounds like. No idea what he looks like. He could be sitting right next to us for all I know."

"But you know it's got to be him who's calling you." Another question. Posed as a statement.

Her new martini comes. She grabs it by the stem, takes an immediate drink.

"Might be better to let it breathe." I smile.

"Eat your steak, Moonlight. And shut up."

"Yes ma'am. You contact the police at all about these phone calls?"

"Mr. Moonlight, I do not wish to bring more attention to my previous mistake than I need to. Besides, what harm can a phone call do?"

"He decides to finally make good on his threats, you'll wish you have contacted the police."

"Please let it go for now, and please go find Mr. Walls."

I nod.

"Okay if I finish my steak first?"

"And by all means finish your beer too. I wouldn't want to deny a Cro-Magnon such as yourself the right to raw meat and booze."

"And don't forget my manuscript."

She shoots me a smile while taking another sip of her martini. "Anything else I can do for you?"

"Don't forget sex with the woman of my choice."

"I never sleep with my clients."

"That mean you're taking on my book?"

"You'd trust me with it, knowing about my sordid past?" She slurs the *S* in sordid.

"Yup. I believe you're the type who never makes the same mistake twice."

"I've been married and divorced three times."

"But not to the same man."

"Naturally."

I dig into more steak.

Suzanne drinks and ignores hers.

For dessert I will get back on the trail of Roger Walls and wallow in the knowledge that not only is Suzanne Bonchance going to represent my book, she's going to sleep with me too.

Chapter 7

SINCE I'VE STILL GOT nearly half a day to kill until I meet up with Erica and her writing professor, I decide to start at the start. That means driving over the big iron and concrete Patroon Island Bridge that spans the Hudson River into Rensselaer County and heading out toward the old town of Chatham, which lies on the hilly, rural borderlands between Massachusetts and New York State.

The drive in Dad's funeral hearse is scenic and peaceful. Miles and miles of the prettiest farm and wild country you ever did see. Soon a stream emerges on the right side of the road. The stream is known as the Kinderhook. A favorite amongst the local fly fishermen. Even I've been known to drop a line in its swift moving, crystal clear water from time to time.

When I come to a short metal bridge that spans the stream and that connects with a narrow country road that leads into town, I pull the hearse off onto the soft shoulder and get out. I spot a lone fly fisherman working the area under the bridge for the trout that might be hiding there amongst the rocks in the shadows. Walking onto the designated pedestrian walkway set along the far right side of the bridge, I stop in its center. I lean both elbows onto the railing and poke my head over the side to look directly down onto the fisherman. For a quiet moment, I watch him work his line with all the skill and grace of a lion tamer and his bullwhip. I don't want to disturb his concentration by shouting out at him, so I wait until he senses my presence and looks up.

"Any luck?" I pose.

"Haven't caught anything but a chill today," he says.

"Maybe they haven't stocked the stream yet. It's early in the season."

The bearded man takes in some line with his right hand while holding to his fly rod with his left.

"An optimist you are. Are you gonna watch or you gonna fish?"

"Neither. I'm working."

"Somebody's got to."

"You from around here?"

"That'd be about right," he says, gearing up for another cast, cocking the nimble rod over his right shoulder.

"You know of a man named Roger Walls?"

He stops his cast, allows the loose line to drop onto the swift moving stream.

"Kind of question is that? Anyone who lives here knows Roger. He's famous."

"Well old famous Roger seems to be missing in action these days and I've been hired to try and find him. Any ideas?"

"He's missing? What are you, a cop?"

"A private detective. His literary agent has hired me to find him."

The fly fisherman smiles.

"You really a private detective?" he asks with a smile. "Or you telling tall tales?"

"Says so on my license."

"You carry a gun?"

I open my leather coat just enough to reveal the inverted butt of my shoulder-holstered Browning .38.

"Nice piece," he nods. "I sometimes deer hunt with a pistol in the fall."

"Any idea where Roger might run off to if given the chance?"

"Can't imagine why he'd run off, unless he shot somebody again." He shoots me a quizzical look. "He shoot somebody again?"

"Not that I know of."

"Must be he's on one of his benders."

"He pull a lot of benders?"

"Good for one or so a year."

"He always leave town when that happens?"

The fly fisherman nods, while once more retrieving his line.

"Almost always. But he always comes back after a week or so, claiming to have no idea where he's been."

If all this is simply about a bender, I could probably camp out in Chatham for a week, collect my money from Bonchance, and wait it out on the comfort of a bar stool until Walls shows back up. Maybe even do a little fishing. But that wouldn't be very honorable of me and I suck at fly fishing.

"Where's a good place to start looking for Roger? In your opinion?"

"How about the tavern? It's the only one in the little village of Old Chatham. Just keep on following the road until it makes the bend at the start of town. It's directly across the street from the post office. Roger has his own stool in the far corner as you walk in the door. There's a bust of him set there too."

"A bust. You mean, like a statue?"

"Yup. Local artist carved it up in clay. Pretty good likeness."

I thought about my own book. If it sold, I wondered if I would ever become famous enough to have my own stool at a village tavern. My own bust.

"How nice for Roger. Must be nice to be famous."

"Can't be that great if he feels the need to get fucked up all the time."

"You got a point there. It's why I avoid being rich and famous myself."

The fisherman laughs.

"Hey, Old Chatham is smaller than small. Blink and you'll miss it altogether. Whether he likes it or not, Roger is one famous writer. And he's our local Hemingway. He brings in much needed revenue from tourists looking to catch a look. Or wannabe writers anyway looking for advice."

"I'll start there. At the stool and the bust and the bar."

"Good luck."

"You too."

He casts his line under the bridge. I hold my position to see if a trout strikes. But nothing happens. What did a famous fisherman say once? They call it fishing because you can't always expect to land a fish with every cast. Otherwise, they wouldn't call it fishing at all. They'd call it, catching.

"Don't give up I say."

"Back 'atcha."

I walk back across the bridge toward Dad's ride while contemplating the fact that I am fishing for Roger Walls. And so far, not a single nibble.

Chapter 8

THE CHATHAM TAVERN LOOKS like one of those ancient American watering holes that might have been frequented by the likes of Benjamin Franklin and Thomas Jefferson back in the day. Maybe the joint they would have come to immediately after scribbling their signatures on the Declaration of Independence and committing high treason against Mother England. Made entirely of rough wood planks and heavy beams, the low-ceilinged establishment is heated by an honest-to-goodness hearth-and-kettle brick fireplace to the left of the door as you walk in. To the right is a long wood bar that is so old, its thick plank top is worn from the countless elbows, glasses, mugs, and bottles that have no doubt occupied it for a century or more.

Just like the fly fisherman told me, at the very near end of the bar as you enter through the wood door, is an empty bar stool sporting a gold-plated plaque that's been screwed onto two of its four legs. Even from where I'm standing just inside the door I can see that the plaque has the name ROGER WALLS embossed into it in thick upper-case letters, as if the name must be presented in a way that resembles the larger-than-life literary legend. Set to the right side of the stool on top of the bar, is a life-sized bust of Walls's bulbous head. It's made of hardened, kiln dried clay, and it depicts the writer's bearded, wide-eyed face as it scowls ferociously at the patrons who occupy the rest of the bar, as if even in his absence, they are nothing but a royal pain in his writerly ass.

There aren't a whole lot of customers at the bar. Two men I take to be spin fisherman drinking tall-necked Buds. Both of them wearing the same green, brown, and white camo overalls and lace-up boots they might wear during deer hunting season, with matching camo baseball hats.

Rednecks.

It makes sense to me that they've gravitated to a place along the empty bar situated directly across from a deer head that's been mounted to the bar-back wall, a Remington lever-action rifle like the kind Hoss used on *Gunsmoke* supported horizontally atop its twelve-point rack. There's a framed black-and-white photograph hanging on the wall below the deer head. It's of a clean-shaven man who's dressed in checkered hunting jacket. No doubt the man responsible for the impressive kill. Possibly the original bar owner, if my built-in shit detector serves me right. Moonlight the master sleuth.

I wait at the bar in Walls's designated spot for a full minute or so, with only the pine wood-burning crackle coming from the fireplace and the mumbled voices of the rednecks to fill the silence. Until a woman appears out from behind a curtain that separates the bar back from an adjoining room. Standing maybe five foot one or two with short, spiked black hair, she bears the stocky build of a country woman who doesn't take shit from anyone, not the least of which would be a drunken, belligerent customer. I peg her for about forty-five or forty-six. She's wearing a plain gray sweatshirt over a pair of loose blue jeans and on her feet, a pair of black pointy-toed cowboy boots. Far be it from me to make any kind of judgment regarding one's . . . let's call it, sexual preference. As far as I'm concerned, whatever anyone does behind closed doors is their own business so long as it doesn't involve kids and so long as they aren't harming anyone. But if I had to guess, I'd venture to say this woman prefers the fairer sex when it comes to getting her rocks off. Something we both have in common.

She approaches without a smile.

"That seat's reserved," she says, her lips hardly moving when she speaks.

"I can see that," I say, putting on the best Moonlight smile I can manage. "Mr. Walls is precisely the reason why I'm here."

She stares at me. Correction. Not at me, but into me. As if on cue, the two rednecks behind her put an abrupt end to their conversation midstream, and glare at me from over her shoulder.

"Okay now that I have everyone's attention," I say after a beat, "my name is Dick Moonlight. I've been hired to find Roger. I'm a private detective."

More silence. More stares. Like I'm an old rusted out pickup they want to tear up for spare parts.

"Tell you what," I say, my eyes focused only on the barmaid. "Why don't I start all over? How about you give me a Budweiser like the kind these fine gentlemen are drinking." I dig into my pocket for a five-spot, set in onto the bar. "I've already had one today. What can one more hurt?"

The barmaid peels her eyes away from me long enough to slide open a cooler and dig out a beer. Uncapping the top with the metal opener mounted to the underside of the bar, she sets it not directly in front of me, but in front of the empty stool beside me to my left. I get the point and shift myself over.

She grabs the five, makes change with it, and sets it down

beside the beer.

"Keep it," I say, trying my best to maintain my Moonlight smile.

"What's this about Roger going missing, Mr. Moonlight?" she begs.

"You don't have to tell this Moonlight asshole nothing', May," barks one of the rednecks. He's the taller one of the two, sporting a black, three-day growth. I can tell he's downed a few already by the way he's trying not to confuse the syllables in his words. "Ain't none of his business." He says "business" like "bishzzznezzz."

"Gospel," chimes in the shorter, chubbier, clean shaven one. "And he ain't showed you any ID neither."

In my head I'm picturing the movie *Deliverance*. Tighty-whitey-wearing Ned Beatty being raped doggy style by two backwoods gangbangers. Makes me yearn for the city life.

I drink down a swallow of beer, wipe my mouth with the back of my hand. Tucked against my ribs inside my leather coat is my Browning .38 caliber. Not that I'm going to need it for anything. But it feels good to know it's there, hanging right beside my broken but still beating heart.

"Well where are my manners," I say, pulling out my wallet, flashing May my laminated PI license. She steps up to the bar, gives it a once over, her lips silently reciting my name like she can read without mouthing the words. "Look good to you, May? All *I's* dotted and *T's* crossed?"

She steps back, looks into my eyes.

"How am I supposed to know? I've never seen one of those before."

I return the wallet to my back pocket, drink down another sip of beer. "You'll just have to have a little faith."

"Hey don't you make fun of, May," Bearded Redneck spits.

"She might be a carpet muncher, but she's one of us. Now isn't that the truth, May?"

She slowly turns to the redneck.

"Call me a carpet muncher again, and I'll cut off your ball sack, Harlan."

"Harlan?" I say. "Never met a real Harlan before."

"Well you just did, wise-ass. So watch your step."

I turn back to the alternative lifestyle abiding barmaid.

"Like I said, May. I'm currently trying to locate the whereabouts of your most famous patron. Would you care to offer up any ideas? Any starting places?"

She crosses her arms over a barrel bosom.

"You're standing in the starting place. Or directly beside it anyway."

"I'm guessing Walls spends a lot of time here."

The two rednecks both break out in laughter.

"That's an understatement," May smirks. "Roger pays my salary. We hurt when he's not around. He attracts a crowd too. And that crowd drinks, especially with Roger's encouragement, because Roger hates to drink alone."

"Then you must have noticed his lack of presence in recent days. Can you tell me how long he's been gone?"

She cocks her head over her right shoulder.

"This time? I'd say about a week and a half so far."

"And if he's on a bender, about how long will he be gone? In your estimation?"

"If it's one of his typical benders, he won't be much more than a week or two before he comes crawling back in, filthy, broke, and not remembering a goddamned thing. He'll sleep it off in the back room for a day or two and then get his shit together over a pitcher of Bloody Marys."

May's story about Walls's benders matches that of the fly fisherman's. Could it be that I'm actually making progress?

"How come he doesn't head right home?"

The rednecks choke on their laughter again. May shoots them a quick look over her opposite shoulder. It immediately shuts them up.

"His wife still lives in the house," she explains, turning back to me.

"I heard he was married again. To an actress."

"Well this is wife number eight, and she's rather young. Maybe twenty-five or twenty-six. Her name is Sissy. She's kicked him out a few times for his drinking and drugging. She's always on him about it, and the more she does it, the worse he gets. The benders become more frequent if he's not writing. And when he's on a bender he can't write even if he wants to."

"So what you're describing here is a vicious cycle."

"Something like that." She shakes her head. "Poor Roger. If it's not the booze that's his own worst enemy. It's the pussy. If only he can learn to keep that cock of his in his pants for a while, he might get down to writing another good book instead of that silly barroom poetry."

"I take it Roger is trapped in another bad marriage?"

More guffaws from the rednecks.

"You can say that again, Mister," offers the clean-shaven one.

"If you had to guess, where would Roger go on one of these benders?"

"Probably Albany," May says. "But you could spend your entire life chasing him from one bar to another and never find him."

"Will his wife talk to me?"

May works up a smile.

"You can certainly try."

"You got an address for casa Walls?"

May shoots another look at the rednecks, as if she needs their approval. The skinny, bearded one glares back at her silently. But his silence is deafening.

"Come on, Harlan, use your words like a good boy. He's gonna find the place anyway. And besides, Sissy will probably chase him off before he gets his first question out of that pretty little mouth of his."

"Pretty little mouth," I repeat, *Deliverance* flashing through my brain again. "Thanks for saying so. I think."

May picks up a pen from beside the cash register, jots down a couple of lines on a Post-It note, hands it to me from across the bar. I pocket it and then finish my beer.

"Thanks for your help," I say, backing away from the bar. "Enjoy the rest of this fine afternoon in God's country."

May says nothing. But the rednecks both grin at me like I'm not a human being, but something that might taste good for dinner roasted over a spit.

"She wasn't lying, Mr. Moonlight," Harlan says as I approach the door.

"I'm sorry?" I say, my left hand gripping the handle.

"You do have yourself a *pertty* little mouth," he mumbles.

I feel my heart pound in my throat, visions of a Ned Beatty down on his knees, his underwear wrapped around his ankles, dancing in my head.

Clean-Shaven Chubby Redneck snorts like a pig.

I open the door and shoot on out like a pig escaping the butcher's blade.

Chapter 9

BEHIND THE WHEEL OF Dad's hearse, I read the address May scribbled down for me on the Post-it note.

16 Pipeline Road.

Sounds like a country address to me, if ever there was one.

I pick up my smartphone, type the address into the Google search engine, thumb send. A map appears. It says, "Get Directions." I do it. Thank God for GPS and digital technology. Otherwise, I might actually have to think for myself or, worse yet, stop at a gas station and ask for directions from a real live human being.

I turn the big eight-cylinder engine over, listen to it purr. Glancing into the driver's side-view mirror, I determine that the coast is clear and pull out onto the gravel-covered road, begin heading in the direction of Walls's spread. Over my right shoulder I can't help but notice an old, blue Ford F-150 pickup truck parked alongside the road. It's got a gun rack mounted behind the seats, at least two bolt action rifles stored there. The tires are thick, off-road, mud chompers. There's a couple of bumper stickers stuck to the rear fender. The first one depicts the red and blue X-shaped rebel flag of the long defunct US Confederacy. Another one says, "How's my driving? Call 1-800-EAT-SHIT." The license plate is a specialty vanity plate. It says, "Free Bird 69."

As I speed up Dad's hearse, I picture my new redneck friends cruising the streets of downtown Old Chatham in that truck, a case of beer set out on the seat between them. I think about being a single girl walking those streets as the truck passes by. Or worse, a lone African American, Hasidic Jew, or Asian citizen. I picture empty beer cans flying out the window, along with a redneck curse only a Neo-Nazi or a Ku Klux Klan member would appreciate.

But then just as quickly, I try and remove the evil thoughts from my brain.

Ten minutes later I arrive at a wooden gate that's attached to a long perimeter fence of wood and barbed wire. It looks like something you might see out west on a cattle ranch. There's a large sign that's been nailed to the top most horizontal board on the rectangular gate. It reads:

Do Not Enter This Driveway Unless You Have Called First! This Means You!

For a brief moment, I sit behind the wheel of the idling hearse and contemplate the sign. In Walls's defense, I can't imagine the horror he must feel when he's trying hard to concentrate on a new book or a new batch of poems only to be unexpectedly interrupted by an uninvited guest. Or worse, the in-laws.

On the other hand, the words on the sign are menacing enough to give me pause. I mean, what if Roger's suddenly returned home and is now standing at the top of the drive, an automatic rifle gripped in his hands? He's already shot somebody once before for having trespassed onto his property. Who's to say he wouldn't do it again, even if it means jail time?

But then, the whole point to this little exercise is that Roger is in fact, not home. Roger is off on one of his benders. Roger isn't home to stop intruders from coming up the drive uninvited anymore than he's around to put a stop to a nosy head-case private dick like myself.

Tossing the hearse back in drive, I pull onto the driveway, and head on through the gate.

The driveway isn't paved. The gradual incline is about a half mile long, both sides lined with oak trees that won't be blossoming for another week or two. At the end of the road is the house. It's a typical two-story white farmhouse with a painted metal roof, single-paned, double-hung windows, and a wraparound porch. Near the steps that lead up to the porch, a two-person swing hangs down from the rafters by means of four chains. The swing is empty, even on a warm, early spring day like this one.

I stop the hearse and get out. I'm not halfway to the porch steps when the front door opens.

"Who the fuck are you?" a woman shouts.

I stop in my tracks. It's got to be Walls's wife. And if it's Walls's wife and she's as crazy as he is, she might just be packing heat.

"I'm sorry," I offer from down on the narrow, slate-covered path. "I know the sign says to call. But I didn't think you'd mind."

The woman is standing inside the open door. From what I can see, she's a small, but nicely curved woman, with thick red hair and greenish blue eyes that laser into me even from where she's perched inside the open door. I'm not entirely sure, but from where I'm standing, it looks like she's holding a beer bottle in her left hand.

"My name is Richard Moonlight," I say. "I understand that

Roger has gone missing. His agent, Suzanne Bonchance, has hired me to look for him."

Silence.

"I thought I would start by visiting his home first."

More silence.

"You're his wife, Sissy, am I right? The actress? You might be able to shed some light on where he went. Plus you must be really worried."

Even more silence. I stand there on the path looking dumb and feeling even dumber.

She lifts her left hand, takes a swig of beer. "She sent you here, did she?"

Referring to someone as Bonchance in the third person instead of using her real human name is never a good sign. But then, what the hell do I know? I'm just the hired hand trying to do my job. It only makes sense that I interview the old ball and chain. Ball and chain number eight, or so I'm told.

"All right, come on up," she says, after a time.

I make it up the rest of the path and climb the stairs onto the porch.

"You want a beer?" she asks, not cordially, but then not impolite either.

"Might as well," I say, watching her turn and head for the interior of the house. "Seems to be the thing to do today."

"Around here it's the thing to do every day," she says, as I step into the house, my eyes glued to her heart-shaped ass which happens to be nicely packaged in the tight Levis. "Night time too."

"Sounds fun," I say closing the door behind me.

"Fun?" she laughs. "You obviously haven't met Roger."

"Not officially, no." I think about telling her about his visit to my college campus all those years ago. But then she'll get an idea of how old I am and she'll figure out that she was probably still a babe in swaddling clothes back then.

"Well then you have no idea just how much fun you're missing, Mr. Moonlight."

"Call me, Dick," I say.

She bursts out laughing.

"I'm sorry," she says through a snort-filled chuckle. "It just sounded funny the way you said it . . . Call. Me. Dick."

Turns out Mrs. Walls is younger than I thought. Young enough to still be into dick jokes anyway.

I follow her into the kitchen at the end of the corridor. Laid out on the counter beside the coffee maker and the microwave is a mirror. It's got cocaine on it, cut into the cutest little white Bolivian marching powder lines you ever did see. An American Express credit card and a rolled up dollar bill are set on the mirror glass beside them.

"Want a blast?" she offers. "Dick." More laughing.

"Usually people offer me tea or coffee when I first enter into their household."

She leans over the mirror, shoves the dollar up into her nostril with the index finger and opposing thumb on her right hand, and snorts up a line like a human vacuum cleaner.

"Tea and coffee is for pussies," she says, lifting some of the coke off the mirror with the pad of her right index finger, rubbing it onto her gums. "Coke is more fun."

She goes to hand me the dollar bill. I've got a piece of hollow-point bullet lodged inside my brain. The last thing I should be doing is snorting coke and getting my synapses into a pulsating turmoil. I am however, working, and imbibing a little might loosen up Mrs. Walls's lips. The lips on her mouth, that is. The things one has to do in the name of good detecting. Moonlight the mercenary.

As usual, Richard Moonlight, is about to make the wrong decision. In the line of duty. I take the dollar bill, head on over to the mirror, and dig right the fuck in.

Chapter 10

BACK WHEN I WAS just a kid—a teenager—my dad used to insist on smelling my breath whenever I came home from a night out with my friends. It's not that he didn't expect me to have a good time and do all those things boys and girls will do when they are coming of age. He didn't mind if I drank a beer or two, so long as I wasn't driving and so long as I wasn't getting in the car with any of my friends who might be drinking and driving. But he wasn't looking for the smell of beer on my breath, so much as he was looking for pot. Dad was a single parent and a conservative one at that. Smoking pot he used to say, was a wrong that would inevitably lead to other wrongs. All it would take is one toke and I'd be heading down that dark, slippery-sloped, heroin-LSD-crystal meth tunnel from which there was no return other than inside one of the Moonlight Funeral Parlor pine boxes. Whether or not dad was way off base about the effects of recreational drugs leading to hard-core narcotics, I never lost sight of the true meaning behind his paranoia. Once you take the leap and make that first wrong decision, it can often lead to other, even more wrong decisions.

Case and point.

Snorting an innocent line or two and washing it down with a couple of cold beers along with Sissy Walls may sound innocent enough, in relative terms. After all, I'm here to get information about where her husband might have disappeared to. And if she's in the middle of doing a little partying, the last thing I want to be is a party pooper. Partiers like it when other people party with them. They like forming a bond with other like-minded people. In doing so, they form loose lips. They talk. A lot. And that's exactly what I wanted from Sissy Walls. Loose lips.

Problem is, those few innocent lines and beers quickly turned into a bunch of lines and a bunch of beers and the next thing you know, we're tearing one another's clothes off all the way upstairs on the way to her bedroom.

An hour later I'm lying naked beside the equally naked Mrs. Walls in her big king-sized marriage bed wondering how the hell I got here but knowing full well it all has to do with making that first wrong decision by snorting that first skinny little delicious line.

"Was it good for you too, cowboy?" she asks, while firing up a post-sex cigarette.

"It was all my pleasure," I tell her. "Believe me. You're a little spitfire. If you don't mind my saying so."

"I don't mind your saying so," she says, setting the lighter back down on the night stand, exhaling that initial nicotine-laced hit of blue smoke. "As you no doubt already know, Roger is getting on in years, and his bedroom performances aren't exactly what they used to be."

"Viagra," I say, not without a chuckle.

"Viagra only works if you're not drunk. It's powerless against whiskey dick."

I turn to get a look at her then. She's lying on her back, staring up at the ceiling, smoking. What I'm witnessing is an unhappy but extremely attractive young woman who no doubt was caught up in the fever of Roger's charm, only to realize a short time later that infatuation is not spelled the same as love. Not even close.

"We've partied and done the wild thing," I say after a time. "And it's been lovely. But I eventually have to get around to the reason for my little visit."

She smokes, exhales.

"Do I have any idea where my husband could have gone?" she sighs posing the question for me.

"That's a good question to start with."

"And his hotshot Manhattan agent just can't rest until she finds him."

"Formerly from Manhattan agent. But yes, she can't rest."

She turns to look at me over her shoulder. "How much is she paying you to lasso him?"

"Enough. Does it matter?"

"Well, I were you I'd get some of that money upfront. She tell you why she wants you to find him?"

"She doesn't have to. Nor is it my business. But she did tell me that she's run into trouble as of late and Roger is pretty much her only client these days. She doesn't get him back behind a typewriter, she doesn't eat. Or something along those lines."

She laughs or, should I say, snorts out her snowflake-chilled nostrils.

"Mr. Moonlight," she says, "Suzanne Bonchance has some money. Some. Money. But not all of it from the sales of her client's books however. Never mind Roger Walls."

I roll over, plant my elbow on the bed, rest the side of my head on my fisted hand. Using my free hand, I snatch the cigarette away from her, steal a slow drag, hand it back. Why is it that everyone smokes when you're trying to quit? Moonlight the hopelessly addicted.

"I'm all ears," I say, placing the cigarette back in her hand.

"Let me ask you a question," she says. "Did you like that coke we just did?"

I'm not sure if I could tell the difference between good coke and bad coke. But I'm not about to let her know that.

"Primo," I say, taking a shot at getting it right. "The best."

"Yup, not bad, right? You know where Roger gets his shit?"

"You mean who he buys it from?"

The invisible light bulb flashes on over my head.

"His agent," I say.

"Hey, New York's top agent has not only fallen from glory with her little literary stealing act, but she's been forced to resort to some alternative bottom-feeding ways of making a living. She tell you about the FBI investigation?"

I picture the Suzanne Bonchance I had lunch with just a few short hours ago. Done up perfectly in a dark suit, not a strand of hair out of place. Maybe she seemed to be sucking down the martinis but she didn't seem to be getting drunk. Despite the slurring of certain words, she seemed pretty much in control. But then she did hardly touch her food. If there's one substance on earth that will kill an appetite, it's Bolivian marching powder.

"She hasn't mentioned it," I admit, remembering how the agent spoke about prank phone calls. Somebody who was out to get her for what she'd done. That someone most likely being the man whose manuscript she stole. Ian Brando.

Sissy stamps out her spent cigarette, rolls over to face me, pulling the covers up over her shoulders like she's only seconds away from closing her eyes and going to sleep. And maybe she is.

"From what Roger has told me, she's been accused of cashing some of her former client's royalty statements, and keeping all the money for herself. That's a no-no."

"I haven't heard anything about extortion. I didn't see anything about it when I did some research on her."

"It's still an ongoing investigation. It isn't public yet."

If what Sissy's telling me is the truth, then either Bonchance is going to have a little bit more explaining to do about her past or I'm going to give some serious thought about first, withdrawing my book from her consideration, and two, quitting my quest to find Roger Walls. For now I'll give my client the benefit of the doubt and chalk up Sissy Walls as a more or less drunk, jilted, and just plain bored young housewife looking to piss on Suzanne while she's down. After all, Suzanne thought it would be a good idea for me to talk with her. If she thought for a second that Sissy would paint the lit agent as a drug running loser, two steps ahead of the cops, she would have insisted I stay away from Chatham altogether.

"I'll look more into it when I have the chance."

"She pay you yet? Give you an advance for your services Moonlight?"

Sissy has a point.

"No. But I rarely ask for one."

"Well, far be it from me to give you advice. You being a professional private *dick* and all." She shifts her hand under the covers, grabs hold of my now sleeping manhood. "But I'll say it for a second time: I'd ask for some upfront money before you waste another second trying to find my drunk husband . . . Cash."

I gently take hold of her hand, push it away from my golden jewels.

"I can take a hint," she says. "Party's over."

"I gotta get to work at some point," I say, sliding out of bed, bending over, gathering up my clothes. The few pieces of clothing that made it up to her room, that is. "So you gonna tell me where you think I should start looking for your husband?"

She rolls her eyes.

"Jesus, do you really have to find him, Moonlight?"

"He's your sig other, Sissy. Don't you want him back, safe and sound?"

A grin forms on her mouth.

"I hate the man's guts, if you want to know the truth. It's peaceful not having him around all the time. Roger is what you call a heavy. It's all about him and him alone. He's my biggest mistake."

I look into her eyes. Eyes that aren't afraid to look away from mine. Sissy is most definitely telling the truth when she says she hates her husband. Excuse me . . . her missing husband.

"He's a writer," I say after a long, heavy pause. "Writer's live in their own selfish world. So I'm told."

"Roger's world is one hell of a place to live in, believe me. It's as vast as it is close-minded and it is hell on earth."

"So where should I start, Sissy?"

"I were you, I'd head back over to Albany, find a phone book, open it up to 'Seedy Joints, Grills, Gin Mills, and Tittie Bars.' Then begin with the *A's*. With a little luck you'll catch up to him by the time you make it to the *P's*."

"That's not a whole lot to go on."

"Hey, you're the investigator. You think of something, Mr. Rockford."

I slip into my underwear and jeans. My tennis socks and boots are downstairs.

"Let me ask you one last question. If Roger is aware of all the shit that Suzanne could be pulling, why does he stick with her? He's a big famous writer. He could have any agent he wants. Why not fire her like everyone else has?"

"If I had a dime for every time I've asked him that same

question, I would have my own place by now . . . In the deep-blue-sea Caribbean, far away from him."

Looks like it's not only Suzanne who's leading a secret life separate from the literary life. Or maybe she and Roger are in cahoots together, partnering up on some serious drug running. But why would a rich and famous man of words take a chance like that? I could press Sissy more about the true nature of Walls's and Bonchance's relationship, both personal and professional, but I decide to let it go for now. I just want to get the hell out of that bedroom and out of Walls's house. I slip my buttoned work shirt over my head, let it hang out untucked.

"Don't bother getting up," I insist. "I'll let myself out."

"I had a nice afternoon, Detective Dick."

"It was rather swell. I'll be seeing you in all the unfamiliar places."

I pull a card from my pocket, leave it on her dresser.

"How poetic. You should think about becoming a writer yourself."

"Thanks, I'll take your advice into consideration. In the meantime, you think of something else beside phonebooks, give me a call. Day or night."

"Maybe I'll call just to call," she says, that grin growing into a full-blown smile. "You look like the phone-sex type."

"Let's not and say we did," I say, reciting one of Dad's famous lines.

"What the hell does that mean?" she begs.

I exit the bedroom at a half-jog without explaining.

Chapter 11

MY SOCKS AND BOOTS back on my feet, I fire up Dad's hearse, and leave the Walls house behind. With my luck, the literary hothead will be heading up into the driveway while I'm heading out. I imagine his gray hair-covered head and thick beard, the exposed skin on his round face turning red-hot with anger. Maybe he'll slam the brakes on his ride, fishtail it in the middle of the drive, making it impossible for me to pass. Then he'll get out, cradling a loaded rifle in his hands. A rifle barrel as deep and black as eternity itself will be the last thing I remember as he blasts me to Kingdom Come. Next thing I'd know, I'd either be riding that wormhole to heaven or to hell, or at the very least, waking up in the recovery room of the Albany Medical Center, what's left of my respiratory system hooked up to some life support machine.

But as luck would have it, I make it to the end of the drive, past the open wood gates and out onto the road without Walls being the wiser.

Thank God for small miracles.

Even though it's possible to catch the highway via a connecting country road not far from here, I decide to head back through town first. Maybe it's possible Walls might have simply shown up in his hometown while I was getting it on with Sissy. If that's the case it would save me the aggravation of having to look for him then beg for my money from a literary agent who just might be dealing drugs on the side while extorting royalties from former clients. Maybe it's the effects of the coke still working on my synapses and nerve endings, but I'm listening to my finely tuned built-in shit detector and it's telling me in no uncertain terms, *Stay away from this one, Moonlight. It's more trouble than it's worth.*

On my way past the tavern, I don't see any cars parked alongside it that might belong to Walls. That's because there aren't any cars parked there at all. That blue "Freebird 69" pickup is gone too. Must be the rednecks it belongs to went back to the woods, crawled back under the rock they call home. Slowing down, I try and get a look through the picture window and into the bar. I can barely make out the bar corner where Walls's bust is situated, but I make it out enough to know that the stool set beside it is presently unoccupied. I hit the gas, and head for the highway.

I'm not a mile down the country road when I spot the redneck's pickup in the rearview.

Chapter 12

IT'S JUST LIKE YOU see in the movies. The fat, meat-eating metal grill of the big truck coming up fast on you from behind. I see the truck in my side mirrors where objects are closer than they appear and I see it through the rearview from the point of view of an elongated hearse that under normal conditions might house a casket of the dearly departed.

Not a great time to be thinking of death.

The truck pulls up on my tail. In the mirrors I see the happy, shiny faces of the two rednecks. One of them smooth-shaven, the other sporting a ratty beard. Both of them hooting and hollering like they just trapped the biggest buck you ever did see. I toe-tap the gas and the hearse lurches forward. Eight cylinders of pure power. But the rednecks probably have a Hemi under the hood of that pickup. They gain on me, come so close I don't know how it's possible that they're not touching my rear fender.

Then I feel it.

The bump.

They ram into my backside and blast their horn. They're so far up my ass I can practically see the black chewing tobacco juice drooling from their filthy mouths. I'm not about to trade paint with a couple of country bumpkins. This is Dad's special ride. His pride and joy. He entrusted me with it, and I'm not about to allow any harm to come to it.

Speeding down the narrow country road, I pull out my .38, tuck it under my right thigh. Then, bracing myself, I hit the brakes while quickly spinning the wheel to the right. The hearse does a complete rubber-burning one-eighty, fishtailing in the middle of the road, the front now facing a pickup turned so hard and abruptly to the left, the entire truck tips up on the right passenger-side wheels. The truck nearly flips onto its side before slapping back down hard on all four wheels.

The rednecks have come to a dead stop, the truck having stalled out.

I slide my foot off the brake and slowly pull up to them, now gripping the .38 in my right shooting hand. Rolling down the window, I cock the hammer back on the .38 while keeping it hidden.

"Looks like we've gotten off on the wrong foot, boys," I say.

"You stupid motherfucker," says the driver. The bearded one. Harlan.

Over his right shoulder, I see the clean-shaven one slowly reaching for the hunting rifle wracked over the seat.

"I wouldn't do that I were you, slick," I say, raising up the .38 and planting a bead on them.

He lowers his hand.

"You come snooping around here again, Moonlight," says the bearded one, "we'll shoot you for real. You got that?"

"If I didn't know any better, Mr. Redneck," I say, "I'd interpret your words as downright unfriendly and non-country-folk-like."

"You just stay away from Mr. Roger Walls, you hear?"

And then it dawns on me. "You two clowns work for him, don't you? You work for Roger."

"What of it? We're his bodyguards. We keep an eye out for him, and he pays us real good."

"Redneck bodyguards. How quaint."

"Screw you, Moonlight."

"Easy chief. We more or less work for the same dude. At the very least we both have the literary geniuses' well-being in mind." Fishing for a card in my pants pocket with my free hand. When I find one, I pull it out, and toss it into the street. "You boys happen to hear anything about Roger and his whereabouts, I should hope you'll give me a call. Day or night. Your future employment might depend upon it."

"And what if we don't, jerk?"

"I'm not sure Roger would like that. Chances are he might shoot ya."

"I'm not so sure he'd like to know about you balling his wife neither."

Maybe it's the effects of the coke wearing off, but his words hit me harder than the grill on that truck.

"I have no idea what you're talking about, Redneck." Pulling back the .38, I hit the gas and pull forward. Making a three-point turn in the road, I head back in the direction of Albany, burning rubber as I speed past the pickup.

Taking one last look at it from the rearview, I see the bearded redneck standing in the middle of the road, bending over to grab hold of the business card. I see something else too. A third head that appears through the pickup windshield. A bald head that belongs to another man who must have been hiding out inside the pickup's cab.

I don't let up on the gas until I make it to the highway. Speed traps be damned.

Chapter 13

FORTY-FIVE MINUTES LATER I'M back in Albany inside my first floor riverside loft. Since it's going on five in the afternoon and I'm still shaking from coke withdrawal and from having been assaulted by two rednecks and their pickup, I decide to crack a beer. Maybe it'll help to calm me down. I've also been drinking all day so I'll make it my last before meeting up with writing prof, Gregor Oatczuk. Moonlight the optimist.

Setting the cold beer down on the butcher block counter, I try to make some sense out of this case. Only this morning was I officially hired to find Roger Walls, but instead of having spent the day on his trail, no matter how vague a trail is it, I've spent my time uncovering evidence that tells me my client and fallen uber-literary agent, Suzanne Bonchance, is a liar and a cheat. Which doesn't bode well for my placing any significant trust in her, not to mention establishing any confidence that I'm going to be paid on time and in full.

I drink some beer. It tastes good.

"So then, Moon," I say out loud to myself in the empty loft. "What have you got?"

I've got a famous writer who left town a week or so ago without leaving a single word to anyone about where he was going or what he was doing. Which in itself doesn't seem to be of great concern to anyone close to him since he's been known to go off on drinking binges for up to two weeks at a time, only to return to his hometown of Chatham broke, filthy, and exhausted. It also further explains why no one has called the police, aside from the fact that Walls shot someone who was trespassing on his property once upon a time and even though he was never convicted and sent downriver, his angry disposition—for lack of a better term—is still fresh in the minds of the boys in blue.

While Wall's wife Sissy clearly hates her husband and is willing to cheat on him at any given opportunity, there is one person in this whole thing who is concerned about Walls and that's the aforementioned criminal literary agent. Which is where this whole thing begins to stink in the first place. Said agent has fallen from her former glory and fallen hard. What once was one of the most respected and famous agents in the industry, has now become a woman scorned. A woman who used to pride herself on an iron fist who could demand the highest bid on any book she was peddling, but who now has been abandoned not only by her entire client list, but by New York City itself—the mecca of literary success. What's more, it's possible she has the FBI after her along with a man named Brando whom she plagiarized.

I might feel a little sorry for Bonchance, but the iron lady has no one to blame but herself. In an uncharacteristic lapse of good judgment, she went and stole a manuscript that she had initially rejected and sold it to Hollywood for six-hundred thousand dollars. Even though she claimed to have simply borrowed the title and some of the idea, it was determined in a court of civil law that she pretty much ripped the whole thing off. But it's not Bonchance's mistake or lapse of judgment that's so bothersome. What I have trouble with is her not having leveled with me from the beginning. And now I find out from Wall's wife that she might be dealing dope in order to make up for lost revenues and that federal agents are on her trail for having cashed royalty checks from some of her former clients.

Okay, I know what you're thinking.

None of this should be any of your business, Moonlight. You've been hired to find Walls and that should be your only concern. Your client's history has nothing to do whatsoever with your objective.

Or does it?

From what Bonchance claims, Walls is the only client she has left. The major question raised is this: Why would someone of his status and world-wide fame decide to stick it out with a known cheat? Why, when everyone else has jumped ship, including the American Association of Artists Representatives, would he decide to stay aboard when the vessel is clearly sinking, if not already sunk?

Bonchance claims that Walls hasn't written anything of significance in ten years. Anything but some poems, that is. Makes me wonder just how rich and famous the writer still is. Money doesn't grow on trees and even the largest bank accounts can dwindle down to nothing if there isn't anything filling it back up from time to time. Something tells me that Bonchance's and Wall's relationship is more than just literary, and that the common denominator might have something to do with two book pros who have known what it is to be on top and now are experiencing the bottoms together. Take it from someone who knows, life at the bottom can be a desperate and black experience. The dime-sized scar beside my right ear lobe and the small piece of .22 caliber hollow-point bullet lodged beside my cerebral cortex is evidence of that.

I drink some more beer, feel the cold, sudsy liquid coat the back of my throat.

I have to wonder if Roger Walls is simply off on one of his typical benders or if he's run off for a different reason, and if that reason has more to do with Suzanne Bonchance than it does his need to skip town for a while in an alcohol-soaked haze.

Maybe his buddy Gregor Oatczuk will be able to shed some light on the subject. If the writing prof claims to know Roger Walls well, then maybe he can at least point me in the right direction as to the author's whereabouts. In theory at least. As I down the rest of my beer, I begin to feel a slight sickness in my stomach. Maybe it's the effects of a big lunch and a dessert of cocaine, sex, and more beer, but the sickness tells me I might not like what I find when, and if, I finally uncover Walls's location. It tells me that I might indeed find the writer, but that the writer might not be alive.

I make a time check.

Five fifteen in the late afternoon. Time to go meet up with Erica and Professor Oatczuk. Crushing the beer can in my hand, I toss it onto the wood counter like Joe Muscles, and exit the loft.

Chapter 14

IT'S BEEN A WHILE since I've driven through the state university campus at Albany. Whoever designed the place back in the late sixties must have had a grudge against anyone who enjoys knowing where they are going at all times. In a word, the place is a confusing maze of parking lots, white, post-modern concrete, glass, and steel buildings that look like they were constructed more for the set of a Star Wars movie than on behalf of educating the youth of the world. The campus wouldn't be so confusingly intimidating if it were made up of only one type of each building. But instead, the planners decided to create four sets of identical buildings laid out in identical fashion on four identically sized flat-land parcels which, when combined, form a perfect giant square. It's confusing because you can park your ride in one parking lot and then later on, mistakenly find yourself searching for it in an entirely different lot that looks exactly the same as the lot you originally parked in. You following me here? You won't realize you're looking in the wrong place until a half-hour or so has passed because the lot and its layout is identical to the three other lots set directly beside it.

In order to avoid the problem of getting lost, I didn't park in the campus parking lot at all, but inside the lot of the Dunkin' Donuts which is located directly across the street from the campus's main entrance. Crossing over the double-laned Washington Avenue, I pat my chest for my .38 which is concealed under my leather coat. I already know it's there, but somehow it feels good just to touch it. Not that I expected any kind of shootout to happen inside the state university campus. But a man has got to be prepared these days. Who knows what a frustrated writer like Oatczuk is capable of when push comes to severe shoving?

Once on the main campus I shoot across the main green until I come to a campus directory that's housed inside a glass case mounted to a concrete balustrade. It tells me that the big white, four-story, concrete-paneled structure set before me is the English Department. Not a very inspiring building for writing new poems and prose. But then what the hell do I know? I was groomed for the funeral business. I grew up looking at stiffs day in and day out. Maybe death is not the most inspiring thing in the world for a young kid, but it seemed perfectly natural to me at the time. Maybe it explains why I had no trouble making the transition to cop and witnessing my fair share of violent deaths while on my near-twenty-year watch. Including my own near death.

I approach the building and make a right around its far corner and onto the main quad of the campus. As promised, my liaison, MFA candidate and young poet, Erica, is waiting for me at our appointed time, her fancy red convertible parked off to the side in the student lot.

"Hope I'm not stealing you away from your muse," I tell her. She's dressed in the same short skirt as earlier, knee high socks under a pair of brown leather boots. Her sandy brown hair is blowing in the wind and her brown eyes are lit up in the bright sun that's beaming onto the open air quad.

"Not at all," she smiles. "I only write at night, when the cool, calm silence makes everything grow still and all right."

"You're a poet and you know it, Erica."

"No lie that I try."

Reaching out, she takes hold of my hand. The feel of her hand wrapped around mine gives my heart a bit of a pleasant start. Moonlight the romantic. Or Moonlight the dirty old man.

"Come on," she insists. "Oatczuk doesn't like it when people run late for an appointed meeting."

"God forbid," I say. "We might make him late for a faculty meeting or something."

Together we head inside the building, take the stairs to the second floor where we enter through a pair of double doors. Erica leads me down a narrow corridor that accesses classrooms and faculty offices. We make it about midway down the corridor until we come to a closed door, a metal nameplate screwed into it bearing the name Gregor Oatczuk in embossed letters.

Oatczuk. Poor bastard must have had a rough time in grammar and high school with a name like that.

Erica knocks.

"Come," exclaims a deep voice from behind the door.

Erica opens the door, steps inside. I follow.

The writing professor is seated behind a big, antique wood desk. He's heavyset, in his late thirties or early forties, and sporting horn-rimmed eyeglasses. He's got a four or five day beard going, and this long, dark hair that's parted over his left eye and draped over narrow shoulders. You can tell he's proud of his hair and the fleeting youth it represents because I'm not through the door for three seconds and he's running both his open hands through it, brushing it back like it's a nuisance. But I can tell he's showing off in front of his student.

"This the man you spoke of, Erica?"

"True dat, Professor Oatczuk. This is Dick Moonlight, honest-to-goodness private detective."

He smiles, stands, points to the free chair set before the desk. "This is certainly a first for this office, Mr. Moonlight." He tells me to have a seat.

"I'll stand, thanks," I insist.

"I like that," he says, settling himself back down in his chair. "A man who is always at the ready. Tell me something, do you carry a gun?"

"Why do you want to know?"

I can see his cheeks flushing under his scruff. He's not used to people answering his questions with a question. He's a professor after all, the master of his fenced-in kingdom. I don't only represent the outside world and reality. As a former cop and now a PI, I am an object of both interest and curiosity to him.

"When I think of private detectives, the ones made famous in genre fiction and the pulp magazines of yesteryear, I can't help but think of guns, illicit sex, and sleaze galore." He shifts his gaze from me to out the window onto the confusing campus. "Mediocre fiction for the masses."

Erica clears her throat. "Mr. Moonlight just wrote his first novel, Professor."

He turns back to me, runs his right hand back through his hair. Nervously. As if the private detective has suddenly become competition instead of curiosity. "You're a multi-talented individual, Mr. Moonlight. What's the name of your opus?"

I glance at Erica. She issues a me a confident smile that screams, *Don't be shy. Tell him.*

"*Moonlight Falls*," I say. "Sort of autobiographical fiction. Or, if you will, Professor, detective fiction meets memoir."

His eyes light up under those horn-rims.

"How interesting. False truths and true falses. A pioneering effort on your maiden literary voyage. How nice for you."

"I wouldn't exactly call it literary, Mr. Oatczuk. More like a mystery novel. Something Dan Brown or Robert B. Parker might write." Feigning a grin. "You know, a book for the simpleton masses. Nothing Roger Walls or maybe yourself might waste your time with." I'm blowing smoke up his ass here, and he either knows it and likes it. Or he's just so used to being creamed on by his students that he expects it.

He nods.

"Let me tell you something," he says, once more gazing out the window. "The other day I had to take the train into Manhattan for a day-long conference along with some of my colleagues here at the university. Something happened that took me by complete surprise. The train was full of readers. Young, old, middle-aged. They were all reading, or so it seemed. Instead of the clatter of text messages being typed, or cell phones chiming, or video games spitting and spurting, people were reading." He sighs as though suddenly deflated. "But then something else happened that would undermine my new-found optimism."

I glance at Erica. She catches my gaze and offers me a tight-lipped nod. It tells me she's more than used to the good professor's pontifications and ruminations.

"I can hardly wait to hear," I say.

"I made a point of trying to find out what the people were reading," Oatczuk goes on. "I actually physically climbed out of my seat and walked up and down the aisle gazing upon the titles of the paperback books. And in doing so, I was sorely disappointed. Because instead of seeing the names of the greats like Tolstoy,

Chekhov, Shakespeare, Melville, Fitzgerald, or Faulkner, I saw only Stieg Larsson, Dan Brown, and even some new writer who used to sell insurance but who wrote a romance novel in his spare time and sold a million e-books. A man who now owns a fucking villa in the Tuscan mountains and a penthouse apartment on Park Avenue in New York." Yet another gaze out the window. "E-books. Can you imagine a world in which books are not printed on paper?"

"Some people would call that progress," I say. "It's a digital world. You don't teach that in MFA school?"

"Give us some credit here. We're not only trying to teach tomorrow's writers how to hone their craft, I believe we're trying to save the written word from the people who abuse it while making millions on their bestsellers and their blockbuster movies."

"I wouldn't mind selling a movie." Nor would I mind a penthouse apartment in New York. Not that I'm about to admit it to Oatczuk.

The professor bursts out laughing, like I suddenly ran behind his desk and started tickling him.

"That's just it, Moonlight," he exclaims, "it's people like you . . . mere pedestrians . . . who pen a first novel and, entirely ignorant of the process, end up writing some piece of subpar material that shoots to the top spot on the Amazon Kindle Bestseller list or some such shit. Suddenly you're being called the next Stephen King or, if you will, Roger Walls. Suddenly you're very rich and famous. And where does that leave real, serious writers like myself?"

"Teaching," I say. "You need to teach in order to make a living."

"Yes," he whispers. "We teach. We have no choice but to teach young adults who have about as much chance of making a living as a writer as I do a private detective."

"Amen to that," I say, my eyes once more shifting to Erica as she nervously bites down on her lower lip.

I know that if I don't begin to steer the obviously bitter Oatczuk off the literary versus genre fiction debate, we might never get to the real reason for my visit.

"Speaking of Mr. Walls," I interject, "I understand you both are great friends. As Erica here might have mentioned, he's gone missing. I've been hired by his agent, Suzanne Bonchance, to find him, escort him back home, and sit him in front of his typewriter so that he might make a little money for them both."

Oatczuk peers up at me from behind his desk. He purses his lips, as if he wants to say something but can't quite put the words together yet.

"So, Oatczuk," I press on, "any ideas on where I might start looking? Since you two are like this?" I raise up my right hand, make a gesture of togetherness by crossing the index and middle fingers.

The professor exhales. Profoundly.

"This isn't about money, Moonlight."

"What isn't about money?" I know precisely what he's getting at, but I'm giving him a hard time. Just because. Moonlight the ball buster.

"Writing. It's not about money. It's about a calling. What we have instead of religion. Or in the place of it anyway. A song inside of us that needs to be sung."

"Which is why you've chosen *not* to make money at it. Isn't that right Oat . . . Czuk."

Out the corner of my left eye, I catch Erica suppressing a laugh by pressing her fisted hand up against her lips.

The prof's lips go tight, his eyes wide, bottom lip a quivering, trembling live wire. A little blue vein pops out on his neck under his chin. The scholarly writing professor has got himself a temper worthy of the mean streets by the looks of things, even though his wardrobe of jeans, moccasins, canvass button-down shirt screams of Vermont, cows, pot, and organic freshness.

"I'm just playing with you, Oatczuk. I know you've been trying to catch a big commercial deal for years now. Suzanne told me so. But things ain't going so great are they?"

"And what business is that of yours, Moonlight?"

"None. But it makes me happy knowing that you know that I know . . . If you catch my drift, Herr Professor." I make sure to say Herr Professor with a genuine German *SS* accent. It makes the little vein on Oatczuk's neck throb all the more. Stealing another quick look at Erica, I believe it's quite possible she's about to pee her little cotton undies. That is, if she's wearing any.

"You consider yourself a funny man, Detective Moonlight. And I suppose you have infused your charming personality into your writing?"

"Almost certainly. Which is why Suzanne tells me she's going to sell it for a million bucks. How's about them apples?" It's a lie of course, but I'm really beginning to enjoy watching that vein throb to the point of bursting.

Oatczuk shoots up and out of his chair.

"You must be joking!" he spits. "Suzanne Bonchance . . . *the* Suzanne Bonchance . . . has decided to take on your book." It's a question for which he already knows the answer, but is having a hard time swallowing. He and his throbbing blue vein.

"Why's that so hard to believe, Oat. Czuk?"

"You my friend . . . you are merely a poseur." He's speaking to me through a bittersweet smile, the fingers on his hands once more combing back that lush hair. "A wannabe. I can bet your talent, or lack thereof, is not even worthy of this writing program. Still, here you are trying to push your first novel through one of the best and most accomplished literary agents this country has ever seen, and ever will see."

"Well now you're hurting my feelings, Professor."

"I believe you are a bald-faced liar, Moonlight. Or, perhaps you did something for her to make her take your book on. It's no secret Bonchance has experienced a rash of poor luck lately. So what is it then? Did you fuck her, Moonlight?"

Erica's jaw drops. It's possible mine does to. But there isn't a mirror around for me to confirm it.

"Professor Oatczuk," I say in as calm a voice as I can work up, "I'm surprised at you. A man of your academic standing and respectability, issuing the f-bomb in front of a student. Tsk Tsk."

He slowly sits back down.

"I truly wanted to help you, Moonlight. But I can see now that you don't need my help. You, your book, your agent, and your attitude may now kindly fuck off all the way out of my office, my campus, and my life."

"*Oops you said it again*," I sing, mimicking a horrid song from an even more horrid pop star from the 1990s. "Sure you don't want to give me at least something to go on that might help me find your good buddy Roger? This ain't about me, Oatczuk, and it ain't about Bonchance, or about you. It's about the safety and well-being of Roger Walls, *New York Times*, *USA Today* and *Amazon Dot Com* bestseller."

"I haven't the slightest idea," he hisses. "Maybe you should talk to his present wife."

"Already been there. She has no clue either."

"And did you fuck her too?"

I find myself shooting a glance at Erica. She returns my glance with a look that says, *Yup, you did fuck her, didn't you.*

"Jeeze, prof, your full of angry f-bombs today. You should write a new poem."

"Yes, fuck you and the fat horse you rode in on. Now, please, exit these quarters."

"With pleasure . . . Oat. Czuk."

I turn, take hold of Erica's hand, just like she took hold of mine earlier.

"And I'm taking your student with me," I add.

"I'll see you at workshop professor," she says, little bits of laughter spurting out between her words.

"I'd like a word with you later, Ms. Beckett," Oatczuk says as we exit his office, closing the door behind us.

Back outside in the common, Erica doubles over in uncontrollable laughter. When she's done, she straightens up, wipes the tears from her eyes with the backs of her hands.

She says, "You are the first person I've ever seen who actually succeeded at putting Oatczuk in his place. You were positively brilliant, Moonlight. " She laughs some more, then adds, "I'm not entirely sure why you chose to piss him off like that, and how good it's going to be for my grades, but it was truly a sight to see. Believe me. But now you still don't have any clue about where to start looking for Roger."

The afternoon sun and its warmth are fading fast, but the absolute relief that comes with leaving the English department behind feels really good.

"I chose to piss him off because I knew from the very second I met old Oatczuk that not only does he have zero clue about Roger Walls's whereabouts, but that he's been lying about being his friend. He's probably met him a few times at college readings and some other university-sponsored events. Maybe emailed with him a few times. Its sounds impressive to his students when he talks about

Roger Walls, his quote . . . 'close friend' . . . unquote." Making quotations marks with my fingers. "But trust me, he's no more buddies with Walls than I am."

"Then why invite you in to offer his help?"

"To make himself look important. Like he's needed. Wanted. Or maybe he's just nosy. Shit, maybe he just wanted to show off his hair."

Erica shoots me a quizzical look with her very young but very stunning eyes.

"It's like this," I go on. "Your Mr. Oatczuk, as good and important a writing professor as he seems, has been trying to break the bonds of the academic prison and become a bestselling novelist in his own right. My built-in shit detector—and it's a finely tuned one I might add—tells me he's a little obsessed with Suzanne Bonchance, Walls's agent. Oatczuk feels that if Roger can be a superstar writer than not only can he be a star too, but he is in fact *entitled* to be a mega-superstar writer. After all, he's a long-haired superstar on the campus of Albany State. It's just a matter of Suzanne giving him the break he needs; a matter of her seeing the light, as it were. Recognizing his particular brand of genius. Maybe he feels that by helping out with Walls, he will somehow place himself in Bonchance's good graces. Hell, maybe he feels she owes him a favor, like taking on one of his books."

We start walking in the direction of the student parking lot under the university common's bright sodium lamplight.

"But why not just try another agent if Bonchance doesn't want him?"

"Because he doesn't want another agent. Even with Suzanne being in trouble, and barely hanging on to her own career, he's obsessed with her representation, simply because she represents Roger. That's what Oatczuk is focused on and obsessed with.

Nothing else will satisfy him."

She stops, turns to me, her face lit up as if she's about to shout out, *Eureka!* "That explains why he got so upset when he learned that Suzanne is going to take you on as a client. He felt he'd been passed up yet again, am I right?"

"Passed up again for an inferior, which only makes it worse. But truth be told Erica, I have no idea if Suzanne is taking me on or not."

"Yah, cause you're not a real writer, Moonlight," she laughs, lightly punching me in the arm.

"What's that, a love tap?" I pose with a wink of my right eye.

Her face turns visibly red.

"Sort of," she says. "You're cute. For an old man who willingly engaged in yucky sexual intercourse with Sissy Walls."

"I'm not old, and I did not engage in yucky sexual intercourse with Sissy, young lady," I lie.

"Sure. Have it your way, Moonlight," she says a little under her breath. "But you are still old. No debating that."

"Not nearly as old as Walls, but just old enough to be your very big brother . . . Sort of."

"Exactly how old are you?"

I tell her.

"Ha!" she barks. "You're like a year older than my dad!"

I paint a frown on my face.

"Don't worry," she says. "Dad and Mom started way young. I was their 'oops baby' when they were still in college. They chose to keep me and grow up fast."

My frown turns upside down.

"I feel better now," I say. "Oops."

"They're still together too, all these years later. That shit would never fly today. Kids are too selfish. Too into themselves and

Facebook."

"True love," I say. "It's Facebook-proof."

"Yes sir," she says. "They are my inspiration, my folks." Pausing, allowing the cool wind swirling around the common to embrace the smooth skin on her pretty face. "So what now, Moonlight?"

"Don't you have some poems to write? Some explaining to do to cute, long-haired Professor Oatczuk?"

"I can write one of those things in my sleep and ah, Professor Oatczuk is rumored to be quite gay."

I find myself smiling at the revelation.

"Now I really feel sorry for all you female MFA students."

"Don't cry for me, Moonlight. You're all man and I told yah I wanna get to know a real private detective. Maybe write something with a plot and everything someday."

"And lower yourself to my standards. Remember, plot is the enemy of the literary novel."

A beaming smile. "Which is precisely why they all put me to sleep," she smirks. "So Mister Detective, it's early in the evening, and getting dark fast. Where, in your expert opinion, should we start looking for Roger Walls?"

"You guys got a phone book around here?"

"I'm sure we can find one."

"We'll look up grilles, juke joints, gin mills, tittie joints, and watering holes. We'll start with the *A's* and drink our way through the alphabet until we find our man."

"That sounds way too fun and way too easy."

"You're right. Finding him will be the easy part. Getting him to come with us won't be."

Chapter 15

WE START WITH THE A's.

In particular, a bar called Aaron's down on Bleeker Street in the west end of the city, near the single-tiered stadium where the Albany Metro Mallers semi-pro football team used to play. Every time I pass by the old stadium I can't help but think of my dad. On any given Friday night in the early fall he might drag me and maybe the occasional date to a game under the lights. The quality of the football wasn't as good as the real pros. Not by a long shot. But it was hard-hitting, and on occasion hard-biting, and I got to eat all the peanuts and popcorn I could stomach. I remember laughing when a punch-drunk player would hobble off the field, remove his helmet and reveal a mouth full of missing teeth. I'd laugh even harder when he'd light up a cigarette and crack open a can of beer while sitting on the bench. Dad would bring along a silver hip flask filled with brandy and let his hair down a little, so to speak. Sometimes he'd even remove his necktie. Something he could never do at the funeral home, working hours or not.

Since Roger is nowhere to be found at Aarons, we keep at it all the way through the downtown *A's*, *B's*, *C's* and *D's*. By the time we get to the *F's* it's nearing midnight, and since we've downed our fair share of beers in many of the establishments we've checked out, Erica and I are starting to feel no pain.

"Wanna call it quits?" I say as we march up Madison Avenue, the lamp-lit Washington Park on one side of the busy street and an endless lineup of four-and five-story brownstone townhouses on the other. "We maintain this pace, we'll end up just like Roger. On a bender that could last for weeks."

That's when Erica does something wonderful. She doesn't answer me with words. Instead she grabs hold of my arm, stopping me dead. It takes me by surprise. First thing that comes to mind is that she's angry with me for something. Maybe for dragging her all over the place on this wild goose chase. Maybe for making her skip dinner. Maybe for making her writing professor look like a fool in front of her. But it turns out she isn't mad. Turns out, she's got something else on her mind altogether.

She presses her young, hard body close to my own, leans into me, and kisses me on the mouth. I might back away, but her mouth is too sweet, her lips too tender, her tongue too interested in playing with my own. I feel myself growing hard and I know she can feel it pressing against her sex. But standing out there in the open sidewalk, with dozens of partiers passing by in each direction, I know this is no place to get it on.

We both break for air.

"You have sugar kisses, baby," I say.

"I've been wanting to do that since we were in Oatczuk's office," she says, her face beaming with happiness. "No . . . I lie . . . Actually I wanted to do it since the first time I saw you in the bookstore."

"I can't believe a beautiful talented girl like you doesn't have a boyfriend."

"I do have a boyfriend. Well, sort of boyfriend. He's at law school in New York."

"When the cat's away," I say.

"What about you, Moonlight? Any serious love interests?"

Lola comes to mind. My true love of a half-dozen years. In my head I see her beautiful long dark hair, her deep-set brown eyes, luscious thick lips, and tan, Mediterranean skin. I can even smell her rose-petal scent. But then I see her lying on her back on a stretch of New York highway immediately after the suburban we are being transported in is rammed by a tractor trailer, and my heart sinks down to my ankles.

"I wouldn't be kissing you if I had one," I say, half believing my own lie. "But, I do see somebody now and again. An artist and an art teacher." In my head my thoughts shift from Lola to Aviva, my newest on-again, off-again. "She's having trouble with the *C*-word."

"Commitment. That can really kill a relationship." Realizing what she just said, and the ease with which she said it, Erica goes wide-eyed and breaks out laughing.

"In a strange way, no truer words have been spoken," I say. "It's okay though. I've been learning to live alone now for a long time. I have a son, you know. He's all I truly care about."

"A boy? How old?"

"His real name is Harrison, but I call him, Bear. He's a good-natured, bushy-haired, ten-year-old. Lives in Los Angeles with his mom. Visits frequently, but not enough."

"I'd love to meet him someday."

Abruptly she pulls away from me, her smile dissolving. She shifts her laser-beam focus from me to one of the many cars parked along the curb.

"What's got you suddenly possessed?"

She turns to me.

"I almost hate to say this," she says. "I've been having so much fun. But I think our search is over, Moonlight."

She takes a few steps forward, raises up her right arm, points with an extended index finger to a silver convertible Porsche Carrera. The parking job is so cobbed that the front driver's side tire is resting up on the curb. A drunk driver, I'm guessing. Moonlight the deductive.

"You're kidding?"

"That's Roger Walls's car," she adds. "I'm sure of it. I remember it from when he came to the university a few months ago for his reading. A silver Porsche Carrera with the back bumper dented in.

Stepping forward, I crouch and take a good look at the rear bumper. Sure enough it's dented in. Like Walls backed into a telephone pole when trying to escape a crowded parking lot, maybe after hitting on jealous man's wife.

"Nice work, depute," I say. "Guess it never occurred to me to ask his wife what kind of car he drives."

"See," Erica says, turning to me, grabbing hold of my right hand. "You need me, Dick Moonlight."

"Question is, kiddo," I say, taking my hand back, "what does a girl like you need with a head-case like me?"

Chapter 16

THERE WAS ONLY ONE bar within the immediate vicinity of the parked Porsche. It was a bar called Ralph's. A local juke joint. Place inhabited by state university and medical students mostly looking for cheap draft beer, good hot Buffalo wings, and a game of darts. The joint took up the ground floor space of a four-story brick building set on the corner of Madison and New Scotland Avenue not far from the Albany Medical Center.

"Ralph's," I say. "It's got to be Ralph's."

"That just seems too damned easy, boss man," Erica says.

"Trust me, it always seems too easy. But in the end, it never is."

"What's that mean?"

"It means, it really doesn't matter where Roger went to hide. That's not the point."

"What's the point?"

"The point is that he might want to remain hidden. That's where the job goes from easy to downright difficult. Especially if he wants to fight us."

"I'm guessing we need a plan."

"Yup."

"Any idea what kind of plan you'd wish to implement, boss?"

"How's this: He resists my request to escort him back home immediately, you take the necessary measures to prevent physical injury to either party."

"And what would constitute actual resistance and specifically what measures might I take?"

"He starts beating the living shit out of me, you hit him over the head with a blunt object."

"Can I use your gun?"

"No."

She paints a false pout on her face.

"Ready for some action, Deputy Beckett?" I pose.

She raises her right hand and salutes me.

"Ready, steady, and willing, Moonlight."

I open up the door to Ralph's and cautiously enter.

Chapter 17

TEN MINUTES LATER I'M down on my knees in a filthy bathroom stall, Walls's bear-like claw gripping the collar on my leather coat. My head is ringing from a quick pistol-whipping, my face and scalp soaking wet now that the literary genius has decided to use my head as a human toilet brush.

He yanks me up and onto my feet.

"Holy crap, Moonlight," he barks. "You passed out on me."

"Pistol-whipping someone in the head will tend to have that effect."

"Sorry about that," he says, making a weak attempt to straighten up the collar on my jacket for me. "I only meant to scare you, not harm you. I don't know who to believe these days. Who to trust. How do I know you're really working for Suzanne?"

"Trust," I mumble. "It's like faith. Believing in something you can't see or feel."

"Indeed. Well said. You're no dummy, Moonlight. Even for a PI."

I run my right hand over my head, do my best to ring out my cropped stand of hair. There's a small lump on the back of my cranial cap where Walls hit me with his six-gun. At least he didn't shoot me. It feels tender to the touch. My poor, bullet-riddled head.

"You got a license for the six-gun?" I pose.

"You're kidding, right?"

"Oh, I forgot," I say. "You shot someone already."

"Convicted felons rarely are granted pistol permits. But don't worry. It's not always loaded. It's more for show, ′case somebody backs me up into a corner."

"Aren't you afraid of getting snagged with an unlicensed piece? It would be immediately prison time. Bullets or no bullets."

"Never shall I be touched by the filthy hands of the man in blue. Never again, believe me, believe you."

More silly poetry.

He opens the stall door so hard it slams against the side panel. The knocking on the dead-bolted door goes from bare-knuckle taps to outright pounding.

"Dude!" shouts the man from outside. "I've got to fucking go!"

Walls shifts his stocky body over to the door, unbolts it, and opens it. An overweight college-aged young man barges in. He's a wearing a tight black T-shirt that says "COLLEGE" in big bold white letters stained with beer and chicken wing sauce. He doesn't bother to look at us while he barrels his way to the toilet I just occupied with my face. Slamming the stall door shut, he drops trou, and slams his ass down onto the toilet. The violent noises that follow remind me of the D-Day barrage on Omaha Beach.

"We'd better get the hell out of here, Moonlight. Get us a drink. Before we pass out from asphyxiation."

"I couldn't agree more," I say following him out. "You're buying, asshole."

Chapter 18

"WHAT'S THIS ALL ABOUT, Mr. Walls?" I ask over a bottle of cold beer paid for from out of the pile of greenbacks set out on the bar in front of the writer. "Why you running when you should be writing?"

"Who says I'm running?" Walls answers, while sipping on a toddy of vodka over ice. A double. "And what business is it of yours, private dick?"

Walls is clearly wired. Tired and wired, not unlike myself, probably due to the same Bolivian marching powder that I've been snorting with his . . . um . . . wife. I've already introduced him to Erica, but an introduction wasn't necessary since he recalls her from the many readings and signings he's done at the university for the MFA program. Truth be told, I was a little taken aback when he first caught sight of her, the big man stopping in his tracks and swallowing a breath. Like she was his mother come back to life and not some kid learning to write poetry. Makes me wonder why she didn't explain the extent of her relationship with Walls in the first place. Why not just come out and tell me she knew him? But for now, I just welcome an excuse to have a couple of calming drinks while trying to get Walls to talk and make some sense out of this goose chase.

"You're right, Mr. Walls—"

"—Roger," he insists. "Putting a 'Mister' in front of my last name makes me feel all literary and snooty. Like Erica's MFA advisor. What's his name again, Erica?"

"Professor Oatczuk," she reminds him, smiling that beaming smile of hers. She's clearly getting a rise out of this whole adventure. And who can blame her?

"Ah yes," Walls says in between sips of his toddy. "Professor Upchuck. Uptight man if I ever did meet one."

"He claims to be your best friend."

Walls bursts out with a belly laugh that seems to light the tavern right up. The bartender and the two kids playing darts over beers in the back stop in their tracks to grab a quick look at Walls, who has no doubt been belly laughing the afternoon and night away in the place.

"So I take it he's not your best friend?" I add, already knowing the answer to my question.

"I'm better friends with my ex-wives, Moonlight, and they hate my guts."

"That's not true, Roger," Erica chimes in. "I know how generous you are to them. Generous to a fault."

He nods, drinks, sets the glass right back down perfectly onto its own condensate ring.

"Indeed," he says contemplatively, "I feel a responsibility to keep them safe and dry even though they have all moved on from my life. Even Sissy, God bless her, is a hare's breath from moving on, making room for Mrs. Walls number nine. Any takers?" He grabs Erica around the waste, pulls her into him.

"Must cost you a pretty penny in alimony and support

payments," I say. "Which leads me back to my original question. How come you're drinking and not writing?"

"And again, my dear Mister Moonlight, how is that any of your business?"

I drink down the rest of my beer, raise up my right hand to grab the bartender's attention. He catches my gesture and heads to the cooler under the bar, retrieving me another one. Placing the new beer before me, I tell him to take the money for the beer from out of the same pile of pretty green.

"You're right," I say. "You don't owe me any explanation. I'm getting paid to find you and now that I've found you, I'm just curious why a man of your talents and responsibilities wouldn't always be putting ass to chair and fingers to keys."

Walls works up a smile, downs his vodka and immediately calls for another one.

"You have a way with words, Moonlight."

"Richard just wrote his first book," Erica adds, sipping on her still full beer, her slender body cozied up to the late middle-aged writer.

The literary lion lights up like a Christmas tree.

"That so, Moonlight?" he barks, his grin turning suspicious. "You looking for me to help you with a book? That's what this is about? That why you been chasing me down like the onset of a stroke?"

"Not at all," I say. "Your agent has already agreed to look at it for me."

"She did? That's very white of her."

"From what I hear, she can use the business. That is, it's any good."

"Yes, the Iron Lady has had a tough time of it lately. She's starting over. Something poetic in that, don't you think?"

"From what I gather, that tough time could have been avoided."

Walls's new drink arrives and he doesn't allow the ice to settle to the bottom before he takes a swig off of it.

"She fucked up and got too greedy even for her," he says wiping his bearded mouth with the back of his meaty hand. "We all fuck up from time to time or so sayeth the good Lord."

"You shot a man," I say, having no idea in the world why I would say it, other than my brain isn't always right.

You would think I just punched the big man in the gut by the way his face goes rock hard, eyes wide and unblinking, Adam's apple bobbing up and down in his throat, jagged purple vein popping out of his forehead.

"Thou shall not refer to me as a killer," he whispers. "That man was trespassing and threatening me with my life. Or should I say, death? Besides, he survived the shooting with a small flesh wound." Now looking away toward the back of the bar, but obviously seeing something very different inside that complicated head of his. "Son-of-a-bitch trespasser probably doesn't even boast a scar at this point."

I calmly take a drink of my new beer, even though I'm preparing to make a run for it should Walls spring up and go after my throat with both hands, or worse, threaten me with another pistol-whipping.

"Easy does it, Walls," I say. "You did what you had to do. I might have done the same thing in your shoes."

I sense a nervousness coming from Erica. She takes a drink of her beer and adds, "Mr. Moonlight almost blew his brains out once."

There it is. She had to go and say it.

Walls assumes a gentle smile again.

"That true Moonlight?" he begs. "You tried to off yourself?"

"Like you just said, we all fuck up now and again. My fuck-up almost cost me my life, and my son his dad."

"How'd you do it?"

"Roger," Erica bursts in. "I don't think Mr. Moonlight—"

"—It's okay, Erica," I say, holding my free hand as if to say stop. "I don't mind talking about it."

"So how did you do it?" Walls presses.

"Twenty-two caliber pistol to the temple." I make like a pistol with my right hand, press extended index finger to the small, still visible scar beside my right ear lobe.

"I don't get it," he says. "Why aren't you dead right now?"

"At the very last second, as I was about to pull the trigger, a vision of my little boy entered into my brain. I began to pull the pistol away from my head. But I was drunk and I hit the trigger. It went off. Most of the hollow-point bullet shattered against my skull. But a small piece entered and lodged itself inside my brain, directly beside the cerebral cortex, making my present life a little bit insecure at best."

"I get it," he says, clearly fascinated. "I bet if that bullet were to suddenly shift right now, you'd fall off that stool and be dead before you hit the ground."

"Something like that." I nod.

Walls is slowly drinking and, at the same time, soaking up my story. It's not the man who just shoved my head into a toilet bowl who's listening right now. It's the writer. I know this for certain when he pulls a small notebook and pen from the chest pocket on his bush jacket, and jots down a note.

"What are you doing?" I pose.

"Hey Moonlight," he says, "didn't you just get through telling me I should be writing?"

"Yah, but I didn't mean about me. I'm writing about me."

"Don't worry," he says, returning the notebook to the jacket pocket, "I didn't say I was going to write a book about you. Just that I'm going to write a book. That is, I can settle on an idea, much less a bloody plot."

I drink a little.

"So maybe that's what this little escape is all about, Roger. Not being able to write. Writer's block."

He inhales, exhales, his beefy chest rising and lowering like the chest on a bull. Running his free hand down his face over his thick beard, he says, "Another brawny writer more famous than me once said, 'When it feels like you're typing with boxing gloves on, it's time to get out of the house. Sometimes for weeks at a time.'"

I find myself nodding.

"Suzanne needs you," I say, remembering what Sissy told me about her having to resort to selling cocaine in order to maintain the lifestyle to which she's grown accustomed. But then, considering the source, maybe that was just the lie of a very angry, and even jealous young and jilted wife. The type of wife Walls seems to pathologically attract. For a brief second I think about confronting him about the cocaine issue and his wife's accusations. But then considering the bear of a man sitting before me, and the inebriated state he's in, and the fact that he's already come close to deliberately killing another man who got on his nerves, I think twice about it.

I slide off my stool.

"I suppose I could ask you to come with us, Roger," I say. "But I'm guessing you're not going to cooperate."

Another one of his beaming smiles.

"Got that right, Moonlight," he says. "And I'm bigger than you. Or, stronger anyway."

"Will you at least call Suzanne, tell her I found you?"

"So you can get paid."

"Yup."

"I'll call her tomorrow. It's late."

I think about her lying in bed, reading my novel. Naked.

"Much appreciated," I say.

"Sorry about the toilet dunking," he says. "If I'd known about your . . . ah . . . cerebral condition, I might have thought twice about messing with you."

"No harm done that hasn't already been done."

"Good luck with your book. And say, would you be opposed to having a drink with me sometime? Under better circumstances? You're an interesting character. I might like to interview you further."

"I just told you, I'm already writing about my character."

"Hey, what's the difference? You have your take and I'll have mine. Besides, my book will sell better."

"I'll think about it," I say. But it's a lie. My story is my story and that's that.

"Don't think too hard. Or you'll end up like me."

"You seem to be enjoying life."

"But underneath this joyous and adventurous exterior, Moonlight, exists a tortured and lonely artist."

"My work is done here, tortured artist."

I turn to Erica.

"Shall we?" I say.

I fully expect her to accompany me back to my ride, and maybe even to my loft. But the MFA student does something that makes my heart sink. She shifts her body even closer to Roger's than it already is.

"I think I'll hang out a little with Roger," she says.

"Yah, we can talk poetry," he says, tossing me a wink of his right eye.

My heart dragging on the floor behind me, I exit Ralph's to go home alone.

Chapter 19

I SLIP BACK INTO Dad's hearse.

It's dark, cold, and black inside and out. Like my mood. Imagine me, Dick Moonlight, Captain Head-Case, getting jilted by a girl young enough to be my daughter for a famous drunken writer old enough to be my dad?

Life ain't fair.

Before I turn over the eight-cylinder, I pull my cell phone from the interior pocket on my leather coat. The little flag that indicates the arrival of a text message appears for me on the screen. I don't recall hearing the little chirpy chime or the gentle vibration that indicates the receipt of a text message. But that's not an unusual circumstance for having been hanging out inside a noisy bar. I press my index finger on the flag and am surprised to see that the message is from Suzanne Good Luck.

I open the message.

Sissy Walls is dead

I read it again.

Sissy Walls is dead

No matter how many times I read those four words, the

message doesn't change.

I spent the afternoon with Sissy.

I drank with Sissy.

I snorted coke with Sissy.

I had sex with Sissy.

Sissy Walls. The wife of Roger Walls. A man who just beat the crap out of me inside a rancid bathroom stall and who shot someone for trespassing on his property.

Now I'm the trespasser, and the territory I trespassed upon is dead.

Fuck me.

Chapter 20

MY HEART PULSING IN my throat, I thumb the dialer and call Suzanne. It's almost two in the morning, but I don't care if she's asleep. We need to talk. She answers after the second ring.

"What the hell happened?" I say in the place of a hello.

"Suicide," she says, not a hint of sleepiness in her voice. "By the looks of it. Or maybe not suicide."

"Who found her?"

"Some men who work for Roger. They called me."

In my head, the rednecks chasing down my tail in their blue *Freebird 69* pickup. "Maybe it wasn't a suicide attempt after all. Maybe she just overdosed."

"Does it matter at this point? Why are you so concerned, Moonlight?"

The thought of telling her the truth about how I spent my afternoon just doesn't seem all that appealing at the present moment. So I just decide to play the concerned client routine.

"Look-it, Suzanne, I found Roger. He's drinking in a bar called Ralph's on the corner of Madison and New Scotland, across from the park. Should I go tell him?"

I make out some shuffling going on in the background. Then, the distinct sound of a snort, maybe the metallic sound of a razor blade being dropped down onto a gilded mirror.

"No, no," the agent insists while sniffling.

"Everything okay over there, Suzanne?"

"Despite the circumstances, yes."

I fire up the engine.

"I'm coming over."

"Now? That means I'll have to put on my face."

"Your face is fine the way it is. We need to talk."

"Fine. So be it."

I ask for her address. She gives it to me.

I hang up and pull away from the curb, picturing the cops who are no doubt scouring the Walls home as I speak. Cops looking for clues, evidence, prints.

Prints and fluids with my genetic imprint on them.

Chapter 21

THE RED AND BLUE neon tubing that cuts through the darkness to spell Ralph's Bar isn't entirely out of range of my rearview when my cell rings. Sliding it back out of my pocket, I glance at the now lit-up screen. I can't say I recognize the number right away, but I peg the prefix as an Albany number. Downtown Albany.

Then it comes to me. The Albany Police Department. My former employers.

I answer the phone.

"Moonlight," I say, trying to hide the alcohol that's no doubt swimming in my voice.

"Richard Moonlight?" the man says on the other end.

"That's me," I say.

"You don't know me, but my name is Homicide Detective Nick Miller. I'm new with the Albany Police department. I was wondering if I could get you to pay me a little visit at the South Pearl Street precinct. Or I'd be happy to come to you."

"When should I come to you and for what?" I say, knowing precisely what it's for, a vision of the young, red-haired bride of Roger Walls lying in bed beside me flashing through my brain.

"It's regarding the death of a woman by the name of Sissy Walls."

The little town of Chatham comes to mind. All the way across the river and into the trees.

"Chatham is a little out of your jurisdiction isn't it, Homicide Detective Miller?"

"That's funny, Moonlight, I don't recall telling you where Sissy Walls resides."

Me. Snagged. Fuck. Fuck. Fuck.

"Now then, Moonlight, since I obviously haven't woken you from out of a sound sleep, why don't we get together for a little chat right now?"

"Do I have a choice?"

"No."

"I'll be there in five minutes," I say.

He hangs up.

I slam my phone down on the empty passenger seat.

Chapter 22

I TEXT SUZANNE, TELL her I'm going to be about fifteen minutes late when I know full well that it might be about an hour or more before I can make it to her house. Maybe two. Maybe never. I'm a former homicide detective. I know how these things go. I also know that if these cops suspect me of fucking with Sissy's life, I'm pretty well screwed until I can prove myself innocent. That might take a lawyer. A very expensive lawyer. But instead of getting ahead of myself, I decide to take a chill, and simply listen to what Miller's got to say. I haven't done anything wrong, after all.

So why should I be worried?

The interior of the Albany Police Department is like the inside of a mortuary and just as pleasant. I know the place like the back of my callused hands. Even the smell that hits you in the face the second you walk through the front glass doors brings you back to a time when your brothers in arms were closer to you than your wife. So close in fact, that your jealous wife felt the need to find comfort in another man who just happened to be one of those brothers in arms I just mentioned. My partner and best friend at that time.

As I walk the narrow corridor to the reception window, I have no choice but to inhale the combination disinfectant and body odor, and I begin to feel a sick queasiness in my stomach. A nausea that has little to do with all the drinking I've been doing or the cocaine I snorted or even the sickening smell of this concrete block and glass building. Instead, it has everything to do with a suicidal past I would rather forget. I hand my ID and .38 to the guard sergeant manning window.

She buzzes me in.

"Welcome home, Dick," she says, not without a snort. Most of the Albany cops aren't very happy with me since I brought down half their house some years ago when I uncovered an illegal organ harvesting operation scheme some of the head cops were running. Everyone knows that cops watch one another's backsides even when their front-sides are up to no good.

The man I take for Detective Miller is standing at the far end of the wide open booking room as I enter. He's not necessarily a tall guy, but he is taller than my five foot nine which is nothing unusual. He's maybe ten years younger than me but a little older around the eyes and, no doubt, in the liver, since most detectives in Albany tend to become prolific drinkers. Clean-shaven, dirty blond buzzed hair, and a neck-tie that's still raised all the way up past his buttoned collar tells me he's all spit and polish, even at two thirty in the morning.

The fact that he doesn't bother to shake my hand tells me he's in no mood for small talk.

"Mr. Moonlight," he says, "please follow me."

"Gladly, Homicide Detective Miller," I say. "I'm familiar with the layout of this fine establishment of law and odor . . . Oops, I mean order." Moonlight the jokester.

He leads me to a small interview room located to the right of the booking room. He opens the door for me, and together we sit down directly across from one another at a metal table under the bright light that spills down from an overhead fixture. His manila file is already sitting out on the table.

"Get you any coffee, Moonlight?" he asks, opening the folder, pulling out some glossy eight-by-ten color photographs. "That beer breath can stop a freight train."

"I had a couple just before you called. In the safety of my own home."

"You always drink alone in the middle of the night? Or is that your first lie since you were no doubt cruising the city?"

"Am I being interrogated about my drinking habits, Detective?"

He sits back, exhales.

"Let's not get off on the wrong foot, shall we?"

"Indeed we shall not." I smile.

"He comes forward again, chooses one of the photos and holds it up for me.

I try not to look too shocked, but I'm not sure I can help it what with the way my mouth goes immediately dry and my pulse starts pounding in my temples. I wonder if Miller can make out my knocking knees.

"You know this woman, Moonlight?"

He holds the picture of Sissy up so close to my face I can practically smell the ink on the digitally printed photo. In the picture she's lying on her bed, face up, her mouth slightly ajar, eyes wide, and lifeless. She's clearly dead.

"She's the wife of Roger Walls. Sissy."

"Very good," says Miller, as if I'm a first grader reading off spelling words. He drops the picture and begins to show me the rest of them, one after the other, which it turns out, are just different versions of the same dead body. Naked, dead body, I should say.

"How'd she die?"

"By the looks of it," he says, "catastrophic cardiac arrest. Perhaps exacerbated by a suicidal overdose or perhaps by asphyxiation."

"Asphyxiation," I say. "You mean like somebody put a pillow over her face and held it there until her heart gave out?"

He smiles. "Jeeze, what a deduction, Moonlight. What a loss you are to this department."

"Thanks. Kind of you to say so."

"Were you by any chance with Sissy today or tonight?"

I sit back in my chair, inhale a calming breath. I think about pulling one of the cigarettes from the emergency pack I keep in my leather coat should I suddenly need to quit quitting–but then think better of it. It will make me look too nervous. Like I'm hiding something.

"Time out, Detective," I say making the familiar referee *T* with my two hands. "Mind if I ask you a procedural question?"

"You gonna ask for a lawyer, Moonlight?" he says. "Because if you are, then screw you. Ain't gonna change anything from my point of view."

"Have you managed to contact the husband yet?"

"We still can't get ahold of him."

"He's a tough one to track down. Take it from me."

Miller gives me a look like he has no idea what I'm talking about. I feel the pounding in my temples grow louder, more forceful while the detective reaches into the file again, only this time he doesn't pull out a photograph. He pulls out a business card. My business card, it turns out.

"This belong to you?"

"Jeepers, isn't that my name written on it?"

He slams the card down, stands. Dramatically, I might add.

"Laugh it up, Moonlight. It doesn't take a brilliant homicide detective to know that you spent some time with Sissy this afternoon. That you drank and did coke with her. And when we find your DNA sample up inside her pussy, we're going to prove you fucked her too. Your prints are all over the house, and the snot from your nose is all over the dollar bill you were using to suck up that white powder."

The pulsing in my head is so intense that I can feel myself on the verge of blacking out. That's the trouble with my damaged brain. Too much pressure can reduce me to a pile of passed out rags and bones. No choice but to breathe in and out, easily and steadily. Evenly.

"Can I go now, Detective? I have this condition with my head."

"I know all about your little, ah, condition, Moonlight. We all do."

"Then you know the seriousness of the situation. I wouldn't want it to get out that you were holding a handicapped man behind closed doors without his formally being charged with anything."

"Should we be charging you with something?"

"I'm not sure. Sissy lived in Chatham which is a million miles away from Albany."

He sits back down, palms pressed down flat on the metal table.

"We're at present working in cooperation with the Columbia County State Police. Chatham is too small to support its own police department. Which is none of your business it turns out."

"Jeepers, as a tax paying citizen, I feel that I'm owed an explanation."

"Give me the truth, Moonlight, and you can go. Did you spend time with Sissy tonight?"

"Her husband has gone missing. Or, *was* missing that is, until I located him tonight at Ralph's Bar. His agent, Suzanne Bonchance, hired me to find him. Thus my comment about him being a hard man to find."

He nods, like I'm suddenly making sense.

I add, "I started by heading out to Chatham to ask his wife some pertinent questions. Simple as that. Routine procedure for a private Dick like *moi*." Turning to the one-way mirror that makes up a good portion of the painted cement block wall to my left. "You get that? *Moi* is French for me, moron."

I turn back to Miller.

"Is it standard operating procedure for you to engage in sexual activity with your interviewees?" he poses, a slight smirk forming on his face.

"You'd be surprised, Miller, especially when it comes to two consenting adults who wish to perform a sexual act together in the privacy of their chosen residence."

The place goes silent for a few beats. It tells me that our interview, such as it is, is over. For now. I should know. I used to be the one sitting across the table from me in Miller's chair. I know the drill.

Pushing out my chair, I stand, turn back to the one-way glass and, raising my left hand and middle index finger high, flip off the audio-visual techie doing the recording.

"Yah, and fuck you too, head-case," comes a muted voice from the great beyond.

I can't help but laugh. Even Miller cracks a hint of a smile.

"Just like old times, huh Moonlight?"

"Let's hope not."

The detective leads me out of the interview room, back across the booking room, and to the door.

"Listen," he says, before the guard sergeant hits the lock release, "if all print and DNA evidence dug up Sissy Walls's home points to you, and you alone, you're gonna need to grab yourself some professional counsel."

I stare up into Miller eyes.

"You trying to tell me I'm suspected of murdering Mrs. Walls, Detective Miller?"

"You know how this works, Moonlight. We find out she didn't die of natural causes exacerbated by drug use, you will become suspect number one. And until we eliminate suspect number one as a viable candidate for the title of crazy-ass murderer, you will indeed remain as such. Clear?"

"Gosh, I'm trembling with fear. I might have to lie down."

He smiles.

"Good to see you maintain a good sense of humor. I like that coming from a dishonorably discharged cop."

"I'm a glass half-full kind of guy," I say.

He nods at the guard sergeant. The solid metal door buzzes, unlocks, and opens automatically.

"Enjoy the rest of your night, Moonlight," Miller offers. "Don't forget to pick up your gun on the way out. And by the way, we got a DWI sweep going on tonight. So I were you, I'd plan on heading straight home to sleep off your little alcohol and drug problem."

I step on through the door praying that Roger Walls still has no idea his wife is dead.

Chapter 23

BACK IN THE HEARSE I make a quick check of my cell phone. When I see that no one has called or texted, I turn the engine over and pull out of the precinct lot onto Central Avenue in the direction of Suzanne Bonchance's townhouse. But shouldn't I be trying to break the sad news about Sissy to Walls? Doing it to his face before he finds out from some greasy cop that I was the last man to be with her before she died? Should I come clean with everything in order to avoid his wrath later on? A wrath that just might involve a firearm discharged in my general direction?

Okay, here's the truth: While my conscience tells me to head straight back to Ralph's Bar for the four a.m. last call in which Walls will no doubt be participating, I make the executive decision to stick with my original plan and make a beeline for my employer. To try and get a handle on the shit storm I've ventured into and to see how I might gently exit from it without being accused of murder, starting with Bonchance agreeing to provide the police with a rock-solid alibi for having met with Sissy this afternoon in the first place.

At this hour, Central Avenue is nearly devoid of automobile traffic. Just the occasional blue and white cruiser speeding past, no doubt prowling for drunken drivers. It's late in the month. Time for the APD boys and girls in blue to make up their monthly quotas. I can only assume Miller wasn't lying about the DWI sweep. I'm more than conspicuous in my big black hearse. Plus I'm more or less still drunk. But I'm not speeding, nor am I taking any more chances now that I'm solidly on Detective Miller's radar. Last thing I need is a DWI bust.

When I reach Bonchance's address on a side street that parallels the Madison Avenue hill in the city's far-east end which is in sight of the Hudson River, I find an empty space across the street and park the hearse there. The entire street seems to be asleep.

Sleep. What a concept.

But when I get out, I can see that Suzanne is still up, at least judging by the light on in what looks to me like the living room. There's a small stone and concrete staircase leading up to the front door, like the kind you might find attached to a townhouse in Brooklyn heights. Pretty soon I'll have been up for twenty-four hours straight. But that doesn't stop me from taking the stairs two at a time. Standing on the landing, my pulse pounding in my head, I thumb the doorbell three times, the sound of an electronic gong coming through the black six-panel wood door.

Suzanne answers the door as if she were expecting me for dinner some eight hours ago. She's dressed in a sheer, white, satin nightgown which supports her substantial cleavage. Her hair is long, dark, lush, and parted neatly over her right eye. In one hand she holds a glass of champagne, and in the other, a lit cigarette—the butt end of which has been fitted into a long, black, plastic filter device. Add to this her fire engine-red lipstick, black eye shadow, and a perfect strand of white pearls wrapped around her neck, and I might confuse her for the return of Yvonne Dicarlo.

"Moonlight darling," she says, just a hint of slur marring her words, "whatever took you so long?"

Without a word, I step inside the door, slam it closed behind me, making her eyes go wide. I grab the glass of champagne from her hand, drink down what's left in it. Then I toss the glass to the floor so that it shatters.

"Yes, Moonlight," she says, "you may have a drink."

That's when I take hold of her arm, pull her into the living room, and toss her down on the couch.

"You are hurting me!" she shouts.

"Tell me what the hell is going on!"

"Whatever do you mean?" She goes for the cell phone set on the coffee table. "I'm calling the police."

I step forward, snatch the phone from her hand, toss it to the opposite end of the couch.

"You've been hiding the truth from me from the start," I say, holding tight to her wrist with my right hand. "Now the police think it's possible I had something to do with Sissy's death."

"How do you know?"

"Where do you think I've been for the past hour? Partying until the wee hours with your star literary client? I was being interrogated by the APD. Homicide Detective Miller to be precise."

"Was Sissy murdered?"

"It's possible somebody tried to kiss her a permanent goodnight by stuffing a pillow in her mouth. And if Albany's finest arrest me for it, you can bet I'm going to let them in on your little cocaine scam. The same cocaine that Sissy was doing when her heart stopped."

Her face goes pale. She tries to pull away.

"Please let go of my arm," she insists.

I do it.

Her cigarette has burned down to nothing—a gray, worm-like length of ash about to drop onto the white shag carpet. "Who told you about the coke?"

"I just told you. Sissy."

"So you *were* with her today."

"Yes, I paid her a visit to see if she had any idea where her husband might have run off to. Nothing unusual about that. In fact, I recall telling you I was going to interview her. We ended up doing a little partying together since by the time I got there she was already on her way to Planet Blotto. Nothing unusual about that either if it gets her to loosen up her lips."

Bonchance grows a sly smile as the ash falls to the carpet.

"Would you be a darling, Moonlight, and get me another drink?"

There's an opened bottle of champagne set in a silver ice bucket on the table by the fireplace. I make my way over to it while she lights another cigarette. I pour her a drink in a fresh glass.

"Get one for yourself too," she says, ever the congenial host. "We need to calm down, think this through."

"I'm good," I say carrying the champagne to where she's still seated on the couch.

She takes the glass in her hand by its stem, brings her red lips to it, and drains half of it.

"Tell me, Moonlight, did you sleep with Roger's wife?"

I don't answer her. I don't have to. She's smart enough to read my face. She's the Iron Lady after all. The master literary agent. Never mind that she's fallen from grace or drunk as a skunk. She's still as sharp as a dagger.

She laughs. "Now I see why you must be worried," she says with a nod. "If the police should happen to suspect you of foul play in Sissy's death and they find nothing but your signature all over the house and, ah, not to mention, Sissy's cute little pink pussy, you just might be heading to Sing Sing. Now isn't that right, Mr. Moonlight?"

"So if the cops come calling to arrest me, you're going to provide them with the alibi I need."

"Which is?"

"That you sent me to her place in order to gather information in the hope of finding her lost husband. Then you will confirm that I left Sissy Walls while she was still very much alive and kicking."

"How do I know that?

"You don't, but you can lie. You're good at lying. You're a literary agent."

"And now, you're a writer. A euphemism for professional liar. Which means, in the end, the police won't really know who to believe, now will they?"

I take a step back knowing that I'm going to get nowhere fast with this conversation. I also steal a moment to breathe. In and out. It's then that I notice the manuscript taking up space on the coffee table. My manuscript. The pages are dog-eared and mussed up, like she's been reading it all night. My heart speeds up. She must see that I'm looking at my book, because she downs her drink and asks me to get her another. Which I do. Moonlight the gentleman.

I pour another glass of champagne, which I drink in one swift pull. Then I pour another for her. Bring it to her.

"Well," I say.

"Well what, Moonlight?" she says, looking up at me with those big eyes.

"Come on, don't play coy with me, Good Luck. What did you think of the book?"

"Come closer," she says, her eyelids falling to half-mast.

She sets her cigarette down in the ceramic ashtray on the table. Taking a quick drink of the champagne, she sets that down too. Then she sets herself back on the couch, running her hands through her thick hair.

I take a step forward.

"Closer," she says.

I step around the coffee table. One more step and I will be kneeling on her.

She raises her right hand and begins to rub me through my pants where it counts.

"Does this mean you liked my book?" I say, feeling myself grow instantly hard.

"You might say that, Moonlight," she answers, slowly unbuckling my belt, then unbuttoning my button-fly jeans, slowly pulling them down.

"I still want some answers, Suzanne. I … need … answers."

"Shhhh, Dick, shhhhh."

She pulls me out and takes me into her mouth, stoking me gently and working me with her tongue and lips. It doesn't take the inevitable very long, and when it happens, Suzanne Bonchance doesn't shy away. She goes for the no mess, easy clean-up version of a perfectly executed blow job. She swallows all of me, hook, line, and DNA sinker. You might think that's when I would take my leave. But she's only getting started. When she stands and slips out of her silk nightgown, the morning sun is just beginning to poke its bright morning radiant beams into the living room. Her cue to take me by the hand and lead me to the staircase.

"My bed will be much cozier than the couch," she says, starting up the stairs.

I watch her naked loveliness climb the stairs and, like Pavlov's dog reacting to the chiming dinner bell, hopelessly follow.

Chapter 24

THE FRONT DOOR SLAMS.

Footsteps pounding up the stairs.

"Where the fuck is he?" shouts the voice.

Roger Walls.

I jump out of bed. Naked. Trembling.

Suzanne pops up, covering her naked breasts with the white comforter.

Walls storms into the bedroom, double-barrel shotgun gripped in both hands. A weapon he must store in the trunk of his beat up Porsche. He's dressed in the same clothing I left him in at Ralph's. Blue jeans, brown cowboy boots, button-down shirt under a ratty bush jacket with the sleeves rolled up. His thick gray hair is mussed and the facial skin beneath his gray beard is beet-red from anger and skyrocketing blood pressure. His brown eyes are wide and even from where I'm standing halfway across the room, I can see beads of sweat dripping off his brow.

"Down on your knees, evil murderer!" he screams, setting the shotgun stock against his right shoulder, planting a bead on me. If he triggers both barrels at me from this distance, he will evaporate my head. I also know that if for some reason the shotgun jams, he's still got that six-gun hidden under his bush jacket. If it isn't loaded he'll crush my head with it.

"Roger, please," I beg, as I lower my naked body down on my knees, my hands raised up in surrender. "I can explain."

"You went to my house. You got drunk and coked-up with my wife. You fucked her and then you killed her."

"Why would I do a thing like that, Roger?"

"Roger, stop it now!" Suzanne finally chimes on. "Put that gun down at once. This is your agent speaking."

He shifts his aim from me to Suzanne.

"Why should I listen to you? You hired this evil murdering scoundrel to chase me down. To defile my wife. To kill her."

"I did no such thing, you jerk. I hired him to find you before you end up killing yourself behind the wheel of that Porsche. You are the only client I've got and I want you healthy and writing. What happened to Sissy was bound to happen anyway. You know what she was like, Roger. You know how she felt about you. Now put that gun down."

He's back to taking aim at me, his chest heaving in and out in deep breaths. The sweat pouring into his eyes.

"Suzanne's right, Roger. I would never harm a hair on your wife's body. I went to the Chatham house this afternoon … well, yesterday afternoon … in order to talk with her about places you might have run off to. Where else am I going to get firsthand information like that?"

"You would have done the same thing, Roger," Suzanne says, backing me up. "You would have interviewed Sissy."

Roger remains silent, those shotgun barrels staring me down like the opaque, bottomless-pit-eyes of the devil himself.

"Did you drink and do drugs with my wife?" Roger spits after a time.

"Yes, Roger. I did drink with her. She offered it up. She also graciously offered me a few blasts. In fact, she insisted on it."

I see the Adam's apple inside his substantial neck bob up and down. The shotgun barrels begin to slowly drop.

"Did you have sex with my wife?"

All the oxygen in the room seems to turn to poison, making it hard to breath. Or maybe it's the effects of my pounding heart and my now paining arms raised up over my head. I know I could lie and pray that I can get away with it. But if my semen is discovered inside Sissy during the internal that's sure to be a part of her autopsy, the police will have cause to arrest me, and Roger will find out the ugly truth then.

"Roger," I say, "I'm so sorry."

I lower my head, squeeze my eyes closed, await the explosion that will send me on my way to an eternity side by side my old man.

But that doesn't happen.

Instead of a shotgun blast, I hear the sound of tears. Soft at first, but then more intense until the sound of crying becomes the sound of weeping. I open my eyes to see the barrels of the shotgun now pointing to the floor while big Roger Walls, tough guy novelist, begins to cry like a child lost in a shopping mall.

He lumbers his way to Suzanne's bed, plops down on the end of it, and lowers his head in defeat. I lower my arms and maneuver myself on all fours, make my way to the shotgun, which I manage to slide out of the writer's sausage-thick fingers without a struggle.

Standing, I open the breaches and pull out the shells, plopping them onto the bed. Then, setting the shotgun back down onto the floor, I slip into my jeans.

"So," I say, turning to the shell shocked Suzanne and the still weeping Roger, "who's up for some breakfast?"

Chapter 25

SUZANNE HAD A CUSTOM outdoor fireplace and stone-cooking hearth built prior to her moving into the downtown townhouse for the purpose of entertaining future clients and party guests. I guess I would now constitute both future client and party guest, even if the party is slightly spoiled for the time being. We do however have eggs and sausage cooking in a black skillet over a roaring fire made from dry pinewood logs.

While Suzanne cooks, Roger and I sit across from one another at a black metal table that's shielded from the warm morning sun by a big umbrella. The burly, macho writer has managed to stop crying for now and pull himself together.

"Truth is, Moonlight," he says, while sipping on a very red and very large Bloody Mary, "Sissy and I didn't have much of a marriage. None at all, in fact. She was screwing everything in sight, as if to spite me."

"There must have been something that brought you two together," I say.

"We had sex on our wedding night, and we had lots of sex before that. But from the wedding night on, nothing. Nada."

I take a drink of my coffee from a thick white mug you might get at a fancy diner.

"How long ago did you marry?"

"Couple years ago, I think. I'm a little fuzzy when it comes to specific dates."

"Why did she marry you if she didn't want to be with you?"

He rolls his eyes.

"The usual story. You happen to meet an attractive young woman in a bar who has aspirations to be an actress. So what do I do? I promise her the part of the leading lady in a movie being made based on one of my novels. On top of that, I promise to introduce her to my agent who has tons of Hollywood contacts and can get her parts in TV shows. Shit like that. Next thing you know she's going down on me in the car outside the bar." He sports a shit-eating grin. "Works like a charm every time."

"Next thing you know you're married," interjects Suzanne, setting a plate of eggs, sausage, and thick rye toast in front of me, followed by another for Roger and one for herself. "And the little woman owns half your estate, which she keeps diminishing daily by blowing it up her nose."

I cut some of the sunny-side up egg and a small piece of the sausage, set it on a wedge of the rye toast, and place it in my mouth. I'm not sure if it's because Suzanne cooked the food outside, but it tastes good. Really good.

"That one of the reasons you went off on a bender, Roger? Because of Sissy?"

He shakes his head, takes a glance over his shoulder at Suzanne.

"Moonlight's in pretty deep, Suze," he says. "Have you told him everything?"

I'm reminded of my having demanded she tell me everything that's going on with this shit storm just before we got slightly sidetracked and decided to try out her bed together. She doesn't answer Roger. Rather, she slowly continues to eat her breakfast. Until she stops, gets up, says, "I'll retrieve the pot of coffee. We're going to need it."

"Grab the pitcher of bloodies while you're at it," Roger barks. "I'm gonna need those."

I pick up the pace of my eating, knowing that the pleasantness of the breakfast is going to be short lived.

Chapter 26

WE FINISH BREAKFAST. ROGER pours himself another Bloody Mary, and Suzanne and I freshen up our coffees. She sits back in her chair like she's trying to catch some serious rays.

"Here's the short and long of it, Moonlight," she exhales after a time. "Roger here and I are in trouble. Big trouble. Perhaps even the type of trouble you might consider life threatening. And trust me when I say it has absolutely nothing to do with a few prank phone calls. That, my friend, is child's play compared to what you're about to hear."

I sip my coffee, listen.

"You see, Moonlight," Suzanne goes on, "after the trouble I had in New York when I was more or less run out of town, I nearly went mad. The literary industry was my life, and I was considered a rock star amongst agents."

"You're still a rock star," Roger breaks in. "The greediest, most ruthless, iron-fisted woman I know."

She smiles.

"Thank you Roger," she says, leaning over to kiss him on his bearded cheek. Then her eyes back on me. "I would have done anything to get back in the game in a big way. That's when I did something I never thought I would have done in a million years."

"She contacted the mob," inserts Walls.

The hair on the back of my neck begins to itch.

"The mob," I repeat. "Italians, I presume."

"No," she says.

"Irish? Jewish? Chinese?"

"No, no, and no."

Now the hair on the back of my neck stands straight up.

"Russian." I swallow.

"Exactly," she says.

"Oh fuck," I say.

Chapter 27

SUZANNE PAINTS AN EXQUISITE picture of how a Russian ex-patriot by the name of Alexander Stalin, a supposed lost great grandson of Uncle Joe Stalin, sent her an idea for a "true crime" manuscript about living with the Russian Mob. He wanted to call it Russian Reign of Death or something intensely clever like that. While Suzanne thought the idea had potential, it would need the hand of a professional ghostwriter. That in mind, she wasn't so sure she wanted to take the project on. Therefore she set the manuscript idea and all of Alex's contact information in the "maybe" pile. That's when the shit hit the fan over the manuscript title she borrowed from Ian Brando and she was run out of town like a recurrence of the plague.

Some months later, after she settled with Brando out of court and knew she had no choice but to move out of the city up to Albany, she met up with Roger to discuss the future of their position in the publishing world. Which, it turns out, wasn't entirely optimistic for either one of them. Suzanne was suddenly without a client list and Roger was still without a manuscript even after ten years of trying to write something. Anything. Anything other than poetry, that is.

What was left of his fortune was being swallowed up by his ex-wives and their support payments, coupled with a new wife who had a taste for cocaine, booze, and other men. To make matters even worse, not only did Roger not have much in the way of ideas for a new novel, but existing sales of his backlist had faded to almost nothing, causing many of his former publishers to pull the plug on any future contracts. In a word, it would take a miracle for them both to fight their way back to the top of the *New York Times* bestseller list. Or the Amazon.com list anyway.

"Enter the Russian mob," I say.

"Bingo," says Roger, draining his glass and quickly filling it up with his third bloody of the morning. "Suzanne agreed to take on Alexander's project with me acting as the ghostwriter in exchange for a little, shall we say, cooperative assistance."

I turn to Suzanne. Look her in the eye.

"Let's have it, Suzanne," I say.

She sits up straight, clears her throat, stares down into the darkness of her coffee cup, as if this will help her remember.

"I asked Alexander if he would be interested in utilizing all his powers of persuasiveness to get me into the good graces of the most powerful publisher in New York."

"The Chance House Publishing Group," interjects Roger.

"Persuasiveness," I say like a question.

Suzanne adds, "My new Russian friends could convince the house's most senior acquisition's editor of signing us on for *Russian Reign of Terror* with Roger as the ghostwriter."

I steal another sip of coffee.

"I don't get it," I say. "Roger's famous. A bestseller. A household name. You are, or were, the most powerful literary agent in the world. Why resort to illegal measures in order to get somebody to publish one book that he's ghostwriting?"

"You mean why sell yourself to the devil?" says Roger, drinking the last of his present bloody and pouring another before he's swallowed what's in his mouth.

"Good question for somebody who has no idea how this business works," says Suzanne. "You see, Moonlight, Roger is indeed a famous writer. But his sales over the past ten years have dried up to a trickle. After his contracts were cancelled, no one wanted to touch him. On top of all this, it's the twenty-first century. Macho, Hemingwayesque writers are no longer all the rage." She sets her hand on Roger's thick arm. "Real men like Roger are no longer seen as valuable commodities. He's a bad boy who wouldn't recognize a politically correct sentence if it slapped him in the ball sack. The type of writer a woman loves to hate."

"And most readers are women," I add.

"Young women," Suzanne agrees. "They love Harry Potter, Amish romance, fantasy, and sexy vampires. Not drunken bar flies who bang loose broads in the back seat of their Chevy then head back into the bar for more shots."

"I like that stuff." I smile.

"You're in the minority," Suzanne says. "The only way Roger and I were going to come back in a major way, was to convince Chance House not only to sign Roger as the ghostwriter for the new book but to offer him an advance never before heard of in publishing. Something that would generate a major media buzz."

"How much were you going to ask?"

"Hold onto your chair, Moonlight," Roger says, taking a drink of his newly poured bloody, some of the red staining his mustache.

"Twenty-five million," Susanne says.

I nearly drop my coffee cup.

"You heard correct. Twenty-five million. Upfront. No

conditions. No contingencies. Finally, literary advances would match those of the sports world. Baseball. Football. Basketball. And half those professional dick heads can't even read at the eighth-grade level."

"An ambitious plan," I say.

"Up until now, the largest advance paid to any single author has been fifteen million. This kind of advance would set us all up for life."

"After the Russians took their cut," I add seeing precisely where this is going.

"The Ruskies were so into it, so convinced they had a deal that would make them famous beyond their wildest dreams, they even offered me a pre-advance," Roger says.

"How much?"

"One million. Cash. Delivered in duffel bags to the place of my choosing, in exchange for a first draft manuscript to be delivered within six months. They would of course provide me with all the research material and interviews via email and internet. It would all be very efficient, of course."

Suzanne sets down her coffee cup. "That one million would allow Roger to write stress-and worry-free. It also would represent about eight hundred thousand more than we would have ever hoped to secure if we had gone about things legally. But once the book was written, and the Russian's forced Chance House into making a deal they couldn't possibly refuse, I'm convinced we would have made history."

A small breeze runs through the yard. It combines with the weighted silence.

"So how's the book coming along?" I ask, knowing I probably just hit a nerve.

Walls looks at Suzanne over his left shoulder. He then lowers his head.

"We hit a snafu," Suzanne says.

"Yeah, a real snag," Roger adds, "the least of which is not making our sixth-month deadline."

"I'm listening," I say.

"I lost the money," Roger says.

Me, shaking my head. "You mean, like you lost it on the ponies? Or the dogs?"

Roger, shaking his head. "No, no. I lost it. Literally lost it."

"Who loses a million in cash?" I say.

"He does," Suzanne says. "The Russians arranged to drop the money off in a couple of individual duffel bags inside two lockers in the Albany-Rensselaer train station, which they did. Problem was, Roger decided to head straight to the station bar for a couple of pops before heading back to my office so we could safely secure the money in safety deposit boxes."

Roger slaps the table top. "It didn't happen exactly like that, Suze. A friend showed up on her way back from New York City. I kindly offered her a drink. She accepted. We had a couple rounds, while the duffels were safely hidden under our table."

"What girl?" I ask.

"Erica Beckett," he says. "The girl you were with last night. Your cute little, um, deputy."

"Oatczuk's perky-titted student assistant," Suzanne adds.

I picture the brown-haired young woman standing me up at Ralph's to be with Roger, even after we'd sucked some face out on the sidewalk. The word *cock tease* comes to mind. But I keep it to myself.

"Did you tell her what was in the bags?" I say.

"I might be a writer, Moonlight," Roger says. "And a drunk one at that. But I'm not entirely stupid. I simply told her I was coming back from a reading in Buffalo, and that that was my luggage. When I got up to take a leak I didn't think twice about it. Who would know what was really stored inside the bags?"

"And when you got back from said leak?"

"The bags were gone," he says, his eyes wide and glistening like the pain in his heart is still intensely profound. "Naturally I asked Erica if she saw anyone take them. But she swore she didn't see a thing."

"How could she not? She was standing over them at the bar."

"Well, yes and no. She too decided to use the lady's room. It probably didn't occur to her to stay with my bags for a minute while I was pissing."

"So what happened next?"

"I searched everywhere. The entire train station. Erica even helped me look. But they were nowhere to be found."

"At first I suspected, Erica," Suzanne jumps. "But then she couldn't exactly have hidden them up her tight little ass."

"Very well put," I say. "And the Russians? I assume you've let them in on your little problem?"

"The Russians were not happy," Suzanne adds. "They lost their money, we're three months past the six months deadline, Roger's drunk most of the time, and they still have no book. And not even the Russian mob wants to put the grease to a Chance House editor if they don't have a manuscript in hand to back it all up."

"They want their money back," I intuit. "They want out of the deal."

"But we have no way of paying it back."

"So?"

"They got creative and came up with some other ways for us to pay them back."

I recall Sissy's coke. How she claimed to have gotten it from

Suzanne.

"You became a dealer for them," I say.

Suzanne lowers her head, stares back down into her coffee cup.

In the back and front of my mind, I'm wondering why the Russians didn't just tell Suzanne to go to hell instead of entering into an impossible deal like she just laid out for me. But then, I was sure it had to have something to do with ego, the desire for this Alexander character to get a book published by the most powerful publisher in the world and written by a famous author, and to have it be the basis for a reality television show. My built-in shit detector was speaking to me too. It told me that Suzanne didn't just present the possibility of Alexander getting published, she promised him publication, fortune, and fame. All it would take on his end was a little mob-like persuasion directed at the publishing house's editor in chief, maybe in the form of a late night B-and-E, the barrel of a .9mm pressed to the temple.

"You didn't just hire me to find Roger," I say, after a time. "You hired me to find him *and* maybe to help him find that money." I'm reminded of those rednecks who tried to rough me up out in Chatham. I recall seeing a third man pop his head up inside the cab when I was racing away. I had to wonder if that third wheel was Alexander Stalin, the Russian mobster and Uncle Joe's great-grandson.

"You're a professional snoop," Suzanne says. "Maybe you can think of something I haven't. We've tried everything. But we can't think of who could have stolen the money. Maybe if you could ask around. Some of your more unsavory friends might know a friend of a friend. Something like that."

"Something like that," I say. "Believe me, if I had a friend who knew about a friend who stole a million bucks, the both of them would be far away from Albany by now."

Suzanne sits back, exasperated.

"Well, at least you got Roger back for me." She stands, her coffee cup in hand. "Listen Moonlight, if you'd like me to pay you what I owe you I'm happy to end our little relationship and relieve you of any further trouble."

"There's just one problem, Good Luck," I say.

She and Roger stare at me.

"The cops think I might have killed Sissy," I say. "And now, from what you're telling me, I think it's possible your Russian friends could have killed her. Either way, if foul play is suspected, I'm screwed."

At the mention of Sissy, Roger starts to cry again.

"So what would you like us to do?" Suzanne poses.

I look into her eyes.

"Help me find a way to convince the police that I'm not the killer. If it comes to that."

"And how in God's name could we arrange that for you?"

"Go to the cops and spill your whole story."

"I told you before, Moonlight," Roger barks. "No cops. They find out what we've been up to they'll put me in prison, no possibility of parole."

"I can't exactly admit to selling coke and being a party to threatening the life of a Chance House editor either, now can I, Moonlight?" Suzanne says. "Not after the calamity I went through with Ian Brando."

"And I'm not about to go to prison for a murder I didn't commit," I say.

That's when Roger raises up his glass.

"A toast," he says. "To us. *The Naked and the Dead and the Totally Fucked*."

Chapter 28

REACHING ACROSS THE TABLE, I grab hold of Roger's Bloody Mary and take a big drink. I slam the glass back down, hard. Blood-red liquid spatters the table like a head shot.

"Jeeze, take it easy, Moonlight," he says. "It's not our fault you had to go and fuck my wife."

Guy's got a point.

I partied and fucked his wife. I've been avoiding that obvious little deviation of SOP for a quite a while now and it's time I owned up to it. In fact, if it weren't for that little, major mistake, I might walk out of there right now with payment in hand, and later on take my chances with the Albany cops. But not me. Not Richard "Dick" Moonlight. Not Captain Head-Case. I might have a little piece of .22 caliber bullet stuck inside my brain where it's lodged directly up against my cerebral cortex. And that bullet might help cause me to make the wrong decision from time to time. But I'm also supposed to be a private detective who is dedicated to doing the right thing. And now that I fucked Roger's wife, and now that she's dead, the least I can do is try and help them find out who might have done it, and while I'm at it, maybe help locate their money. Which is exactly what I offer up.

"But I don't come cheap," I tell Suzanne. "My fee just doubled. And if I locate the money, I'd like a bonus."

"Such as?"

"You take on *Moonlight Falls* as my official agent. No questions asked."

She smiles.

"I was going to do that anyway, Moonlight."

"Congrats Moonlight," Roger says, holding out his hand, "you just scored the best hard-core tight ass, pussy shaved agent in the business. Plus you got a blowjob and a little doggy style for a signing bonus. Jeeze, you must have some lit skills after all."

I let the hand go ignored.

"I have a question," Suzanne says. "With Sissy's body no doubt in police custody, how in the world are we going to arrange preventing the police from suspecting you or Roger as the killer?"

Roger lowers his hand slowly.

"We're going to do the impossible," I say.

"How's that, Moonlight?" Roger begs.

"We're going to steal back Sissy's body," I say. "And then we're going to make it look like a certain Russian mobster killed her."

Chapter 29

OKAY HERE'S THE TRUTH: I have about as much chance at locating that missing million bucks as I do winning the Nobel Prize in Literature. I might be wanting to do the right thing here to make up for my tryst with Sissy, but I'm also not about to head to prison. That will take enlisting these two fallen literary angels to help out with my cause. If they can help with stealing Sissy and arranging her body to appear to have been killed by someone in possession of fingerprints and DNA besides my own—especially those of a Russian thug—it might at least place a semblance of doubt in the minds of the cops as to who actually killed her. That alone would get me off the hook. And if I could do so under the pretense that I am also working on locating their money, they might be willing to help me out, even if the body we're about to steal is Roger's wife.

In the meantime, I decide that it might be time to place a call to my old friend and spiritual brother, Georgie Phillips, retired Albany Medical Center pathologist.

I do it.

Georgie comes on the line. I picture the long, gray-haired Vietnam vet sitting in his living room parlor, a little Hendrix going on the stereo, the vintage vinyl record spinning on the turn table while he rolls himself a fresh joint.

"Moonlight," he says. "To what do I owe the pleasure?"

I explain everything to him.

"I can get you the private viewing if we head there now," he assures me. "This early in the morning the joint will be as quiet as a—"

"As a morgue," I say. "Funny."

"But this little plan of yours," he adds. "It'll be highly illegal."

"Never stopped us before," I say.

"True ´dat, Moon," he says. "I can expect the usual payout?"

"For your grandkid's college education," I say. "Absolutely."

"I'll pick you guys up in my van. Be ready in ten."

"We're ready now," I say.

He hangs up.

That's when my cell phone vibrates with a new text message. I thumb it open, stare down at it. It's from Erica Beckett. I'd almost forgotten about her. To say that I'm troubled regarding the young poet's intentions is putting it lightly. Her being a major cock tease is the least of it. Why didn't she tell me how well she knew Roger? Why not just be open about it? And now I discover that she was present the day he lost all that money. Even if she didn't steal it, something isn't right here, and I intend to confront her about it the first chance I get.

I read the text. *How is Roger? I'm worried.*

I thumb a text back in. *Hanging in there. How was your night?*

Fun. Until we found out about Sissy.

It occurs to me that Roger didn't have a cell phone on him, and that no one, aside from Erica and I, knew where he was, much less the police. Far as I know, news about her death hasn't yet gone out on the wire.

I thumb in another text: *Who told you she was dead?*

I wait for a response. Until I get one.

I miss you cutie. Heading to bed. Long night. Long morning. ;)

How did you find out? I text once more. But again, I get nothing in response.

I try and call, but all I get is her answering service. "Hi this is Erica . . . You know what to do . . ." Her voice screams of confidence, youth, and beauty. But I'm beginning to suspect something else.

I pocket my cell just as a white Ford extended van pulls up

My bro, Georgie Phillips, to the rescue.

Chapter 30

INTRODUCTIONS ARE QUICKLY MADE and within a few minutes we're piled into Georgie's van. Suzanne rides up front while Roger and I occupy the back. Georgie is driving. He's wearing his usual uniform of Levis straight leg jeans, cowboy boots, black all-cotton T under a ratty jean jacket he's probably owned since high school prior to his being shipped off to Viet Nam. His long gray hair is tied back tight in a ponytail and his clean-shaven face is tanned from the sun, even though technically speaking, he's supposed to stay out of the sun since being diagnosed with skin cancer.

On the way to the hospital, George asks for our undivided attention while he goes over the plan to steal Sissy. When he's through, he focuses his ice-blue eyes in the rearview so that he can get a look at Roger.

"I've read all your books, Mr. Walls," he says. "I was a big fan in college after ´Nam. I thought you nailed the pure, raw, male, sexual character better than Norman Mailer or Henry Miller."

Roger looks at him and smiles.

"Thank you, Doc," he says. "But I'm afraid there's not a

very big market anymore for what I'm doing. If there was, Sissy wouldn't be dead, and we wouldn't be in this mess."

"Who knows?" Georgie says. "Maybe you'll get a new book out of all this."

"That is your pal, Moonlight, doesn't write it first."

Suzanne turns, shoots me a smile and a wink. Suddenly, she's back to her old confident self.

"Maybe we can both take a shot at writing it," I say. "But let's hope we're not doing it from a prison cell."

"A prison cell might be optimistic," Roger says. "I don't locate that money then I just might find myself not writing anything from six feet under."

We make it to the Albany Medical Center in five minutes flat. Because we need to drive around the back in order to access the morgue, we're required to enter the campus through the delivery entrance which is manned by a guard shack. Obviously security at the AMC isn't exactly paramount, that is judging by the overweight attendee who barely fits inside the glass booth. But that doesn't stop Georgie from insisting that we make ourselves invisible. Without argument, Roger and I crawl into the empty back-bay, with Suzanne following on our tails.

The former pathologist stops the van outside the shack.

"Nice to see you again, Doctor Phillips," says the overweight man behind the glass. "You coming back to work?"

"Good to see you too, Brian," Georgie says, as he's handed a laminated clip-on badge. "Just doing a little freelance work. Helps pay the bills." He signs his name to a sheet of paper that's stuck to a clipboard, then hands it back to the guard.

"Enjoy the morgue," the guard says.

"Seems like everyone is dying to get there," Georgie says with a fake laugh.

Tapping the gas, Georgie drives into the heart of the campus, past the main hospital, then the medical college building, and past the physical plant on our left. Soon we come to a series of concrete docks, the last one of which is set beside a pair of extra wide electronic sliding double-doors. Georgie makes a three-point turn, then backs up slowly to the doors. Attaching his laminated badge to his jean jacket, he opens the door to the van, and slips on out.

"How much money you got?" he says.

"Which one of us?" I say.

"All of you."

I shovel through my pockets, come up with three crumpled up twenties, some dollar bills, and some loose coinage.

"Seventy-three and change," I say.

"Come on," Georgie presses. "Who's got some real money?"

"Maybe we should have hit a cash machine on the way over," I say.

Both Roger and Suzanne are going through their respective pockets.

"Nothing," the literary agent says. "Not a dime."

But then Roger raises his right hand high while lying on his side on the van's metal pan floor. The hand is squeezing a folded stack of bills. "Five hundred plus," he spits.

"Jesus," I say. "Leave it to the broke bestseller."

"That should last Roger a couple of days at the bars of his choosing," Suzanne chimes in.

"I might have more in the other pocket," adds Roger.

"Just slip me two hundred," Georgie insists. "Now. Please."

I take the money from Roger, slip out two, one hundred dollar bills and hand them to Georgie who takes them and closes the door. Then I hand the rest of the money back to Roger.

"Plenty left over," he says, repocketing the cash into a chest pocket on his bush jacket. "We should probably stop at the liquor store on the way home. Pick up some supplies."

We wait.

Minutes tick away like hours.

I decide to kill some of the time by pressing Roger for more info.

"Those two rednecks I mentioned before. The ones who threatened me. They really work for you?"

He nods.

"Yeah," he says. "Mostly they do maintenance around the house. Mow the lawns, do the shopping, things like that. Sometimes they try and act like my bodyguards even though the only fighting they've ever done is on Nintendo. I let them do it anyway. Gets them off. Makes them feel important."

Once more I tell him about the third man who popped his head up inside the cab. How I *swear to God* I saw a third bald-headed man when I was speeding away from the pickup truck. Saw his reflection in the rearview mirror.

"No fucking way," Roger insists from down on the van floor. "Those guys always work together and alone together. They're retarded like that. Maybe even queer. Not a chance anyone else would be with them. Especially some asshole who's hiding."

"It could have been the Russian who wants the money back. Alexander Stalin. The one who wants you to write his book, make him famous."

"No way," Roger repeats. "Those dumb rednecks aren't even aware of the existence of those Russian freaks. And vise-versa."

"Doesn't mean it can't happen," Suzanne says in my stead.

"I still don't believe it," demands Roger.

I would argue further with him, but that's when I hear the doors to the morgue open back up, and the sound of a heavy gurney being wheeled out.

One of the van's back-bay doors opens. Standing outside it is Georgie. He's positioned at the front end of a gurney that's got a black body bag set upon it. The body bag is filled with a body. Presumably Sissy's. At the foot of the gurney is a young African American male dressed in the button-down shirt and pants of a morgue orderly. Now I know the reason for the two hundred dollars. Those orderlies make squat while expected to clean up after the dead. Literally. Georgie, who is both Pathologist Emeritus at the AMC and a former carjacker in another life, knows precisely who to grease on the inside and who not to grease.

"Shift over everyone," he insists.

We do it.

Georgie takes a quick step back while the black man pushes the body forward into the empty space on the van bay floor. My stomach turns at the thought of the dead Sissy Walls now pressed up against me in that cold body bag.

The bay door slams shut.

The gurney is wheeled back through the morgue doors while Georgie repositions himself behind the wheel of the van. Turning the engine over, he shifts the transmission into drive and pulls out, heading back in the direction from which we came.

Impossible bodysnatching mission accomplished.

Chapter 31

BACK OUT ON THE open road, I sit up and breathe a silent sigh of relief. But then, I also half-expect a cop to pull up on our tail, hit the flashers and sirens. I can hear the headlines broadcast over the airwaves now:

"Murder suspect also charged in body snatching plot. Details at the top of the hour."

"How on earth did you manage to grab Sissy's body?" Suzanne asks Georgie while she snakes herself back into the front passenger side seat.

"It's not all that difficult," Georgie says while pulling onto Madison Avenue which will take us up to the street where his townhouse is located. "If you have full authorized access to every nook and cranny of the hospital including the morgue, you can pretty much take what you want. So long as you return it in a reasonable amount of time. How do you think it was possible President Kennedy's brain went missing during his autopsy in '63? In Sissy's case here, she was already bagged and stored inside the cooler. She'd even been assigned her own gurney. It was just a matter of wheeling her back outside and into the van."

"Isn't she scheduled for an autopsy soon?"

"Tomorrow afternoon at three to be exact. Says so on the charts and on her toe tags."

"What if the schedule changes and somebody shows up to find that there's no body?"

"That's where luck comes in. Plus, my examination won't take all that long, and we'll have her back in place in the morgue cooler in a matter of three hours. Maybe less."

Georgie turns onto his street. It's then, inside the relative silence of the van, that I hear it. Crying.

I turn and see that Roger is lying beside the body-bagged Sissy. He's hugging her, his face jammed into the nape of her neck, tears streaming down his round white-bearded face and onto the black poly.

"I can't believe it," Suzanne whispers after a time. "All she did was screw around on him, tell him to his face how sorry she was for marrying him. How she had zero feelings for him."

"Love works in mysterious ways," I say.

"So does grief," adds Georgie pulling up to his townhouse, thumbing the button on the overhead garage door opener. When it's opened all the way, he slowly pulls the van inside and closes the garage door. Killing the engine, he slips on out of the van.

"Okay, people," he says, coming around to the back of the vehicle, where he opens the back bay door. "Time to find out what happened to Sissy."

Chapter 32

GEORGIE AND I OCCUPY his basement laboratory while Suzanne and an upset Roger elect to hang out upstairs in the living room. The work Georgie is about to do is not pretty, but then it's not the least bit unusual for Georgie or me. I grew up with this stuff. Dead bodies were an everyday sight for me. Some of the bodies that came my dad's way were not very pretty. Car accidents. Gunshot wounds. Stabbings. Facial mutilations, contusions, and crushings from head-on collisions.

Once—and I remember this like it happened three minutes ago—we received a decapitated body that belonged to a construction worker who'd fallen from a high scaffolding tower and onto a metal fence. Imagine a nine-year-old boy waking up in the morning in his Batman and Robin pajamas only to head on down to his dad's embalming room where a badly bruised and battered headless body was lying on the gurney while its head rested on a stainless steel tray on the counter beside it. Meanwhile, my dad feasted on his morning ham and egg sandwich, a tall Dunkin' Donuts coffee set directly beside the head, the wall-mounted television tuned into *Good Morning America* and some recipe they were trying out for a low-calorie Sloppy Joe.

"Morning son," my dad barked in his usual Moonlight Funeral Home cheer. Then, while taking a bite of his sandwich and aiming his thumb over his right shoulder. "Do me a favor and hand me that, would you, kid?"

I remember taking a few steps toward the head, my pre-adolescent stature just the right height for me to stare the head directly in the eyes. Which were wide open and dark brown. The expression on the face was pure shock, like the head knew that it had been detached from its better half just before it died. The face was round and sported a three or four day growth like lots of construction workers who don't care what they look like on the job. The hair was thick and black, mussed up and caked with dried blood. I raised up my hands and, not knowing where to take hold of the head, grabbed hold of both ears.

That's when my dad nearly scared the pajamas off of me by issuing a loud belly laugh.

"Not that!" he exclaimed, his mouth full of ham and egg. "My coffee!"

The body lying on the gurney in front of me now couldn't be more different from that mutilated construction worker from forty years past. The naked Sissy Walls looked just as beautiful and sexy as she did when I shared a bed with her less than twenty four hours ago. Only difference now was that her skin was cold and pale, with some marbleization having taken effect, mostly in the legs. SOP for the newly dead, especially for the female gender, whose skin is somewhat thinner than a man's.

I watch while Georgie makes a cursory examination of her body, careful not to make any lasting marks on her skin while he pokes and prods at her flesh with an extended index finger covered in a blue latex glove.

"So let me get this straight," he says after a time. "You had sex with her, and you did a few lines and had some drinks. She had already been partying?"

"I'm guessing that, much like her husband, she is the type to never stop. Only when she passes out and can't help but take a break."

"What's that they say about opposites attracting, Moon?"

"Clearly not in this case. Only reason she still looks so good is because she's young."

He pokes and prods her scalp with one hand while pulling back sections of her long red hair with the other. When he's finished, he stands upright.

"I gotta be honest," he says, pulling off the rubber gloves, tossing them into the medical waste bin beside the stainless steel table. "I ain't seeing anything here that tells me somebody messed with her other than herself. No bruises. No scrapes. No scratches. No cuts or lacerations of any kind. Not even in the scalp."

"Evidence of an injection?"

Shaking his head.

"Not that I can see. And I would most definitely see the familiar target-shaped, round purple bruise and black pin-prick center on a girl whose skin is as light as hers."

"So what do we do?"

"I guess it's possible someone forced her to somehow ingest a whole lot of drugs. But then, from what you tell me, she was already doing this?"

"What if someone poisoned her?"

"Takes tox exam to figure that one out, and I most definitely cannot do that here."

My eyes glance at her neatly groomed sex.

"Can you clean her up for me?"

"Yah," he says, nodding gently. "I can get rid of anything that proves you were the last to be with her within hours of her death. But you probably don't want to hang around to watch, even if you're not the squeamish type."

"I don't."

"Why don't you head upstairs and catch the local real-time news on the computer. See if your face shows up. Then we can figure out your next move and make plans for getting Sissy back to the hospital."

"You're a good pal, Georgie."

"Don't mention it. Just another little adventure in illegal pathological examinations in a long list of illegal examinations."

"Naturally."

I go for the stairs that lead up to the living room.

"Moon," Georgie calls out, as I take the first stair.

"What is it?"

"Those two train wrecks upstairs. Bonchance and Walls. You really trust them? They telling you everything?"

I exhale, then breathe in the odor of disinfectant and alcohol.

"Look who we're dealing with here, Georgie. A man who makes shit up for a living and a woman who sells all those lies for big money."

"Enough said," Georgie frowns. "Watch your back."

"No truer words . . ." I say, and head back up the stairs.

Chapter 33

UPSTAIRS IN THE LIVING room, I check my cell. Two calls from Detective Miller at the APD. Two messages to go with them. I decide not to listen to them yet while I head for Georgie's laptop computer which is set up on the same long table where he stores his 1970s-era Yamaha stereo-cassette system and turntable.

Since the laptop is already opened, I just click on the spacer and the Google search engine appears for me like magic. I type in Channel 9 News which is the local Albany real-time news network. Real-time, meaning it's updated every hour on the hour.

My stomach drops as soon as I click on the site.

My face appears for me in all its full-color glory. It's not a bad shot actually, snapped when I was still a detective at the APD. I had more hair then. It was darker too. I sported an equally dark mustache and goatee. My brown eyes screamed of optimism, along with hopes and dreams that had yet to be shattered. Not exactly the face of someone who now is a suspect in the death of the wife of local *NY Times* bestselling author, Roger Walls.

From behind me I hear the sounds of Roger and Suzanne in the kitchen. I make out the unmistakable sound of the top being popped on a can of beer. Roger has obviously raided the refrigerator and discovered Georgie's stash of Budweiser tall boys.

I read the small article that goes with my picture.

The story tells of Sissy's body having been discovered in her Chatham home by two workers under the employ of the Walls family whom I take to be the rednecks from the tavern. After examination of the premises it's apparent that Sissy was doing drugs and alcohol, possibly with myself since not only was my calling card found on the scene but so were my prints. Said prints are easily traceable via the Albany Police Department database since I not only used to be under their employ but I currently collect a half-pension from them.

Go figure.

Detective Nick Miller is then quoted as saying, "While we still haven't arrested Mr. Moonlight, we are currently requesting that he surrender himself to authorities for questioning."

Now I know the reason for his phone calls.

The piece finishes up by saying that the deceased's husband has been missing for more than a week and a half and is still missing. While Walls was arrested in the early 1980s for having shot a man who trespassed on his Chatham property, he is at present not being considered a suspect in the case of his wife's death should it in the end, turn out to be something other than natural causes.

So there it is.

Roger is off the hook for his wife's death while all the fingers point to me. I know that soon, the AMC pathologists will go to work on Sissy and when they do, they will not find my semen inside of her. But that won't exactly prove that I didn't kill her, will it?

I sit stewing while I listen to the sound of Roger pontificating on the nature of death and its inevitability. Suzanne smokes, listens and no doubt worries her pretty little head off over recovering that one million in cash she owes the Russians.

That's when it comes to me.

The Albany cops have been looking for a way to nail me for something for years, ever since I brought their department down over that Mickey Mouse illegal body parts op they were running. I know that if even the slightest possibility of my having aided in Sissy's demise exists they are going to try and at least nail me with manslaughter. I've seen it happen a hundred times before. At the very least, a person who is doing heavy drugs with another person bears a responsibility to prevent that other person from ingesting too much. It's possible they are going to try and nail me with aggravated assault and negligence and try their damndest to put me in Sing Sing for a couple of years or more. When it comes to the death of a high profile figure or in this case, the death of the wife of a prominent world-renowned author, someone will have to pay.

That someone is me.

Here's the deal: We can either return the body right away and I can take my chances on the APD clearing me of all charges. Or we can hold onto her for a just a little while longer and make certain that her body of evidence will in fact, prove that I didn't kill her.

How am I going to accomplish the impossible?

I'm not going to do it alone.

The great-grandson of Uncle Joe Stalin is going to help me.

Chapter 34

I SLAP THE LAPTOP closed and race back down into the basement lab, explain my plan to Georgie.

He looks at his watch.

"She's scheduled to go under the knife at three," he says. "That gives is us about four hours to pull this little stunt off."

I make some quick calculations in my head. Forty-five minutes to Chatham. Which means there goes an hour and a half driving time right there, giving me only two and half hours to meet up with Alexander (assuming he'll meet up with us in the first place) and to make it look like I wasn't the last man to be with Sissy prior to her death after all. I don't have to prove he killed her. Just that he was there. That alone should raise enough doubt in the mind of the police to let me off the hook. Considering he's a member of the Russian mob, while I'm known around Albany as a mostly law-abiding head-case, that should shift the focus of their investigation away from me and onto him and his band of merry Russian men.

"The way I see it, Georgie," I say, "if Alexander meets us on time, we can pull this off in just a ten minutes or less."

"How do you figure that?" Georgie asks.

"Ten minutes is the average time it takes the average couple to complete the act of sexual intercourse," I say.

Chapter 35

WHILE GEORGIE BAGS UP Sissy along with a few necessary tools of the trade, I stand with Roger and Suzanne in the kitchen.

"I thought you were going to help us get our money back, Moonlight?" Roger begs, slurring his words just a little as he finishes off his third beer since we arrived at the townhouse an hour prior.

"One person is already dead, Richard," Suzanne presses, lighting yet another cigarette. "We need that money." She's beginning to develop some black and blue bags under her eyes. Her hands are trembling slightly. I can't help but wonder if the literary agent turned coke dealer is now suffering from the DTs.

"The money isn't going to be a problem," I say. It's a lie, but not entirely a lie. If I can manage to get this little legal problem behind me, I will be free to look for their money. Even if in the back and front of my mind I firmly believe that it's long gone.

"How so?" Suzanne begs.

"You call Alexander for an emergency meeting," I tell her. "You explain that you don't have the money yet. But then, that's okay, because you don't have to pay him back now that Roger is home and sober and has written his book, as originally agreed upon. Now you want to see him face to face, so that you can personally hand him Roger's book. You want to prove to him how excited you are to work for him. How wonderful and thrilling his story is. How handsome and courageous he comes off in it. How this whole thing has been a terrible misunderstanding."

"But he'll know we're lying since we haven't done any research. It was supposed to be a part of the deal. Driving around Manhattan and Albany in Alexander's big black Lincoln listening to details about which wise guy he knifed under which bridge or which mobster's head he decapitated in which basement."

Me, shaking my head, once more picturing that severed head hanging out beside my dad's large Dunkin' Donuts coffee in his basement embalming room.

"Just tell him that Roger did enough research on his own through initial interviews, emails, and the World Wide Web to come up with a very nice first draft. Stress the point by telling him that's how Roger works. And now that the first draft is done, you desperately need Alexander to read through it as soon as possible so that Roger can begin on the second draft and the two of them can begin their on-site research."

"I see where you're going with this Moonlight. If Alexander thinks we're producing a working manuscript, then he won't threaten us with bodily harm if we don't give him his advance back. We'll be honoring our original agreement even if we are way past our original deadline."

"Exactly."

"I'm not entirely sure I can write sixty thousand words in just a few minutes, Moonlight," Roger chimes in, laughing and popping the top on another beer.

I look over one shoulder and then the other. I catch sight of the

Georgie's printer. There's several reams of paper stacked underneath the table.

"Roger, you come with me," I say. Then to Suzanne. "In the meantime you call Alexander and arrange the meeting."

She takes one last hit off her cigarette and stamps it out.

"I'll do my best," she says, pulling her iPhone from the pocket inside of her jacket. "What have I got to lose but Roger's life and my own?"

Chapter 36

I ONCE MORE OPEN Georgie's laptop. I go to Microsoft Word, request a new document. A blank page comes up. I push out my chair and stand.

"Would you like to do the honors, Roger?"

The big man is hovering over the laptop.

"You want me to sit down in front of that thing?" he says, like he's about to be re-introduced to a sweet old lover who jilted him a long time ago. And he is.

"You don't have to do much," I say. Then I tell him exactly what to write as if he doesn't already get what's going on by now.

Slowly, almost painfully, he sits down into the chair. He sets his beer down off to the side on the table. Lifting his big beefy hands he sets them on the keys and I swear I can smell the salt coming from the tears in his eyes. Tears that at present, are staining his beard.

He begins to type. Two-fingered style. One letter at a time.

Click Clack. Click Clack.

He picks up a little speed prior to fingering the enter key, which is the modern-day equivalent to slapping the metal bar on an old manual typewriter after you've come to the end of a line and now require a new line to type on.

He types some more.

Speedy now.

You can almost feel the heat oozing from his pores. The energy emanating from an artist who's been caught up in an almost permanent hibernation for months or many years, but who's now being reborn.

When he's done, he issues an exhale and does something amazing.

He smiles.

His face is positively beaming when he comes down on the return key once more and pens one final, third line. The line completed to his satisfaction, he gets up, opens up his arms and throws them around me.

"I'm sorry I used your head like a toilet bowl brush," he bellows. "You are my friend and my savior. Even if you did fuck my wife."

He's crushing me in his bear hug, his tear-soaked beard rubbing up against my face.

"My pleasure, Roger," I say, through constricted lungs.

Out the corner of my eye, I look down at the screen.

It reads:

Russian Reign of Terror: The Story of Joseph Stalin's Great-Grandson and Life with the Russian Mob

by

Alexander Stalin

with

Roger Walls

Chapter 37

THE PRINTER IS ALREADY connected to the computer via a USB cable. While I print out the title page, I grab hold of one of the stacks of paper, tear off the paper packaging. I muss the paper up a little bit, bending some of the ends to make it look like it's been handled by big dirty fingers for a period of weeks. Then I set Roger's title page on top of it. Retrieving two thick rubber bands from an unused ashtray that's filled with paper clips, pens, and pencils with the tips broken off, I wrap them around the paper stack. One horizontally and then other, vertically.

I set the "book" down onto the table.

I'll be damned if it doesn't look like the real thing.

Drinking down the rest of his present beer, Roger glances down at it. "Did I write that?" he says, his face still beaming with an all-teeth smile.

"You know what, Roger?" I say. "You goddamned well did write that."

"The magic is back, Jack," he sings, as if believing without a doubt that he truly did write a brand new novel.

I turn to Suzanne who is now standing in the living room, her iPhone in her hand.

“Well?” I ask. “Alexander? Is he in?”

“He’ll be there in forty-five minutes.”

“Can the present day Stalin be trusted, Good Luck?” I ask.

Suzanne’s frown turns upside down.

“He’s a killer and a drug dealer, Moonlight.”

“Oh yeah,” I say. “There’s that.”

I go to the basement door, open it.

“Georgie!” I shout. “Grab the girl and let’s move out!”

Chapter 38

WE ALL PILE BACK into Georgie's white van. Roger takes the shotgun seat since it's his house we'll be driving to. For obvious reasons, we'll take the scenic route over the most out-of-the-way country roads we can find. Some of the roads unpaved.

I sit in back with Suzanne and for the first time, listen to Detective Miller's messages. As I suspected, he's asking me to surrender myself for further questioning now that they have Sissy's body in custody at the AMC morgue. If I don't respond to his request by three o'clock today, he'll consider me fleeing his demand and he'll officially issue a warrant for my arrest. He also tells me that although they haven't gone public with any of their findings, a preliminary examination of Sissy's body suggests foul play. Obviously that initial exam occurred before we stole the body.

"If we find your man chowder floating around up inside her, Moonlight," he adds, "God help you."

Man chowder . . .

I have to wonder if Albany cops require a negative IQ in order to be employed. But then, I was a cop once. I should know. Or perhaps they changed the rules since the unexpected initiation of my so-called retirement.

Hitting the number seven on my keypad, I delete both messages and silently pray that we can pull off our little plan for Sissy and Alexander Stalin and have her back in the morgue by three o'clock.

We enter into the town of Old Chatham, Roger leading us on a maze of narrow, gravel-covered roads that bypasses the little village entirely. I'm sure he'd love nothing more than to make a pit stop at his favorite tavern, but that will have to wait.

Time check.

Twelve noon.

We have at best an hour and a half to pull off my plan and then pack Sissy back up and get us all back on the road to Albany. Arriving at the Walls's driveway, the first thing we see is that the front wood gates are cordoned off by yellow crime scene ribbon. It looks slightly less formidable than Roger's "Keep Out" sign nailed to the fence post.

Not wanting to mess with the ribbon, Georgie puts the van in park and gets out, leaving the door open. Gently he peels away the ribbon and allows it to drop to the dirt road. He then gets back into the van and pulls into the open gate. He stops the van once more and replaces the ribbon, like we never drove in here in the first place. Leave it to Georgie, master pathologist and detail man.

Slowly we make our way up the drive, knowing all the time that not only will Alexander be in the house waiting for us, his goons will no doubt be eyeing us the whole way.

"Just because you can't see them, doesn't mean they won't see you," Roger points out.

"You're preaching to the choir, Roger," I say, feeling for the .38 holstered under my left armpit. "I've had a bellyful of experience with the Russian mob. We go back a long way."

Suzanne turns to me, sets her hand on my leg.

"I know you do," she says. "You wrote about them in *Moonlight Falls*. You're lucky to be alive."

"Depends on who you're talking to," I say.

We pull up to the house and Georgie kills the engine. I hand Suzanne the fake novel while remaining out of sight in the back of the van. Georgie remains behind the wheel for now to act as Suzanne's official driver.

"Go," I say. "We don't have a lot of time."

"What are you going to do, Moonlight?" Roger says, opening his door.

"You'll know what I'm doing when I do it. Just play it for real. You have the first draft of his book and you're delivering it to him for his approval."

"And what if he demands to read it on the spot?" Suzanne begs while opening her door.

"He won't have time," I say. "Just go."

Suzanne and Roger exit the van and begin making their way to the front door. As they walk, I hear Roger say, "I hope Sissy didn't drink the joint dry."

Chapter 39

"READY, GEORGIE?" I SAY.

"Sure you wanna do this, Moonlight?" he begs. "It's creepy."

"Don't worry," I say. "Sissy is gone now and it's all for a good cause. Besides, look who we're about to be dealing with. A Russian mobster who claims to be directly related to Uncle Joe Stalin. Stalin killed more innocent people than Hitler. Only reason no one ever heard about it is because he was an ally."

Georgie reaches into the glove compartment, pulls out two lengths of rope, and a tube of KY jelly. He makes a swift little underhanded pitch and tosses the items onto Sissy where they settle on top of her black body bag.

I pull out my .38, open the van door and step on out while zippering up my leather coat.

"You take the front door, Georgie," I say. "And I'll take the back. Let's do this before she starts to smell."

Georgie pulls out his own .9mm, thumbs off the safety, slips on out of the van and starts jogging to the front door. If anyone has had their eyes on us, there's no doubt about our intentions now, which is why I need to move fast.

I pop out of the van and sprint around the back of the house. I immediately spot a big wood deck that wraps itself around the entirety of the big farmhouse's backside. I recall the back door that leads into the kitchen, I climb the stairs onto the dock, head straight for it.

Transparency reveals the truth.

Before I even get to the door, I can see what's happening through the floor-to-ceiling kitchen window. Suzanne and Roger are down on their knees. Suzanne's shirt has been ripped off, along with her bra, her pert, pale breasts exposed. The man standing directly over her is dressed entirely in black. He's got his pants pulled down around his knees and he's making her take him in her mouth, while he's forcing Roger to swallow the barrel on what looks to be a chrome-plated .44 Magnum. The kind *Dirty Harry* used to carry. The hammer is thumbed back on the pistol. The thug's trigger finger is tickling the trigger while Suzanne is sucking him off. If the metal gun is truly loaded with real live bullets, it's possible that trigger finger is going to retract when the fleshy gun shoots its own particular load.

Even from where I'm standing outside the window, I can almost see the beads of sweat pouring off of Roger's brow. I can feel the agony in Suzanne's tears. The literary duo have no choice but to kneel there and take it. Standing behind the goon I take to be Alexander are two more Russians. Both of them dressed in identical black outfits. Black jeans, black leather coats, black shoes, black sunglasses. Gripped in their hands are identical .44 Magnums, one bead a piece planted on Roger and Suzanne. If Alexander doesn't get them, the backup squad will.

I see Georgie enter into the picture. He's made his way quietly from the front vestibule down the short hallway to the kitchen. No one seems to have noticed his presence yet, which is exactly the way I want it. I've got a choice here: I can either try and negotiate with the mobsters, or we can cut to the chase by focusing on the rescue of Roger and Suzanne.

I vie for the latter.

I grab Georgie's attention through the plate glass window. I raise the two fingers on my left hand to indicate the number two. Then, with the same fingers closed together, I point them in the direction of the two goons on the backup squad. He gets my meaning, flashes me a single raised finger on his free hand. I then pat my heart, meaning, "Don't kill them. Just shoot to wound." He nods in total understanding. Georgie and I have known one another as close as two non-biological brothers can for nearly forty years. We don't need to speak directly to know what each other is thinking.

My left hand held back up, I stick up three fingers.

"One," I mouth, dropping the first finger.

"Two." Dropping the second.

"Three."

I hear a shot, just as I burst through the door. At the same time, I fire the .38 at the legs of the backup goons. They never get a shot off before they drop on the spot, the blood from the wounds in their thighs already spurting blood. Alexander is on his back, the .44 still gripped in his right hand. He gets off a shot that shatters the chandelier over the kitchen table. It falls from the ceiling in a resounding crash.

He's screaming "Shit! Fuck! Motherfucker!" in Russian-accented English.

I kick the other .44s out of reach of the wounded men and nearly break my big toe doing it.

"Drop it!" Georgie screams. "Drop the gun!"

He fires again, the bullet hitting the ceiling, plaster reigning down on his still erect penis.

Suzanne is screaming. Roger is still on his knees. He's grabbed hold of Alexander's still stiff manhood and he looks like he's about to yank it off. His face is so red with rage I'm afraid he will.

I lean down, press the barrel of my gun against Alexander's forehead.

"Roger, let it go!" I scream. "We need him and his dick."

He issues me this scrunched-up-brow look of confusion.

"Get his gun," I add.

Roger does it, turning the barrel back onto the thug.

"What are you going to do to me, motherfucker?" Alexander begs, the wound in his lower shin draining blood like a bad leak. His face is pale with pain.

"We're not going to kill you yet," I say. "We're going to finish what Suzanne started."

The look on his face shifts from pain to disgust.

"What kind of creepy, perversion man are you?" Alexander spits.

"It's perverted, Alex," Roger corrects, standing back up on his two feet. "It's per-ver-ted. If you're going to say it in English, say it right."

"Alexander," Suzanne says, pulling her black T-shirt back over her head, tucking it into the waist of her jeans. "Meet my newest client. Mr. Richard 'Dick' Moonlight. Part time author, part time private detective, full-time hater of the Russian mob."

Chapter 40

AFTER BINDING THE WRISTS and ankles of the two Russians I wounded with my .38, I ask Roger to stand guard over them.

"What are you doing with Alexander?" Suzanne asks.

I hand her one of the other two hand cannons the thugs brought along.

"Georgie and I are going to interrogate him inside the van," I lie. "You help Roger."

She seems a little apprehensive at first, like she doesn't quite believe my story. And for good reason. As a woman who sells fiction, her built-in shit detector must be as good if not better than my own. She's also read my book. Which means she's fully aware of how much I hate Russian mobsters and now, how desperately I need to clear myself of having anything to do with Sissy's death. But that doesn't mean I want her to witness what Georgie and I are about to do.

Before Georgie and I proceed to carry Alexander out to the van, I make sure Roger has himself a couple of cold beers sitting out on the kitchen table and that Suzanne has a fresh pack of smokes and a mirror with some neatly cut lines laid out on it. Courtesy of Sissy

Walls. God rest her soul.

"Ready Georgie," I say, hefting a woozy Alexander to his feet, with his left arm wrapped around my shoulder.

"Don't pass out on us, Mr. Stalin," Georgie says, pulling a vial of Viagra from his jacket pocket. "We need to get that hammer and sickle in the mood."

Chapter 41

WE HAUL THE WOUNDED thug out to the van where we shove him into the back cargo space along with Sissy's body.

"What the fuck are you doing with dead body?" he begs in heavy Russian accent. "Get me away from dead body."

While I'm standing outside the open cargo bay doors, Georgie jumps inside, sets himself onto his knees to the right of Sissy's black-bagged body. He pulls his cell phone from the chest pocket on his jean jacket.

"Here you go, Alex," he smiles, holding out the phone toward the wounded Russian. "Why don't you call the police and tell them what's happening."

The thug coughs up a luggie, spits it in Georgie's general direction. The pathologist might be nearing his senior years, but he's still quick on his feet. Or, in this case, his knees. He shifts his head out of the line of fire as the thick wad of spit splats against the van's hollow metal wall.

Sufficiently pissed off, Georgie, pulls his .9mm, presses the barrel against the goon's forehead.

"Get undressed," he orders.

Georgie unzips Sissy's body all the way, revealing her pale, chalky face and mussed up red hair, along with the entirety of her naked body.

There's a look of profound confusion mixed with pain and fear on Alexander's clean-shaven face. His steel gray eyes are open wide, brow scrunched. His mouth has gone dry, judging from his incessant swallowing and the way his Adam's apple bobs up and down in his throat like a turkey awaiting the axe.

Georgie tells me to hold my gun on the thug while he returns his to his shoulder holster. He then unzips his duffel bag, pulls out a bottle of Poland Spring Water, uncaps it. Hands it to the Russian.

"Hold this," he says.

From outside the open doors, I hold the .38 on the Russian, pointblank, safety off.

Alex takes hold of the water bottle.

"I play a doctor in real life," Georgie goes on, pulling the vial from his jean jacket pocket. "I want you to swallow these." The old pathologist pours a fistful of pills into the palm of his hand. He immediately attempts to transfer the pills to the Russian's hand. But the Russian tosses the water bottle at Georgie's head.

"Fuck you, pig!" he screams.

Georgie turns to me. "Moon, shoot off one of his big toes."

Without hesitation I press the barrel of the .38 against the goon's boot tip.

"Wait! Please! Fucking wait! Stop!" he begs.

Georgie, still holding out the pills. "Well, what's it going to be Alexander Stalin? This is one of those you-can-do-this-the-easy-way-or-the-hard-way moments."

I push the gun against the tip of the boot so that he gets the point. He winces in pain since the foot I'm messing with belongs to the shin I've already put a hole through. He takes the pills from Georgie and pops them down his throat. The entire handful. Reaching around his backside, Georgie retrieves the water bottle and hands it back to him. Half the water is gone, but he swallows what's left along with the pills.

"What is in pills?" Alexander begs as soon as he can get his air back.

"Viagra," Georgie tells him. "You've just taken enough to make an elephant hard as a rock."

As if on cue, we all shift our glance in the direction of the thug's junk. As if it's about to rise like a muffin inside an Easy-Bake Oven.

"You are insane, da?" he says. "That many pills will make me kiss bucket."

"It's 'kick the bucket,' Alex," Georgie corrects. "Kick, the fucking bucket. And I don't really care what happens to you after you give us a sample."

"What sample?" the goon begs.

"Your sperm sample."

"I do no such thing."

He's moving now. Shifting his body as if his already too tight clothing is growing too uncomfortable for him. The pills are working.

"Yes you will," Georgie tells him. Then Georgie tells him precisely how and where he wants that sperm sample delivered.

The goon's face goes from pale to purple. For a split second I think he might throw up. Georgie pulls Sissy's legs out of the body bag. She's limber and rubber-like now that the rigor mortis stage of death has passed. He positions her legs like she is about to give birth and, reaching back into his kit, pulls out a pair of blue Latex gloves, slaps them on. Next, he produces a tube of K-Y Jelly. Squeezing a dollop out onto his finger pads, he applies the K-Y in the required area. Then, his eyes on Alex, he says. “Let’s go Romeo. Batter up.”

“Batter up. What does that fucking mean? Batter up. You mean like dick. Dick’s up?”

“It’s just a saying,” Georgie says. “Let’s go, assume the position and make it happen.”

But the goon backs away. His look of horror turns to weeping. He begins crying real tears. The tears are streaming down his cheeks.

“Please. Don’t make me do this.”

“Let me ask you something, Alex?” Georgie says. “Did you enjoy raping Suzanne? Making her suck your cock while you stuffed the barrel of that pistol into Roger’s mouth? You weren’t crying then.”

“It was all in good fun.” He smiles. “Like building of Berlin Wall.”

“Good fun.” Georgie laughs. But nothing’s funny. “How many men and women you killed in your day, Mr. Stalin? How did you kill them? Shoot them in the head? Did you rape the women before you killed them? Did you cut their heads off? What about the boys you’ve tortured and killed? Did you cut their throats? Do it in front of their mothers?”

Alexander remains silent, knowing that Georgie isn’t exaggerating. Like me, Georgie has had his share of near-death run-ins with the Russian mob.

“I have never made anyone do the wild thing with dead people before,” the thug wails. “That is going against unwritten rule. Like disobeying Geneva Convention or something.”

“First time for everything,” Georgie insists, tearing off his rubber glove and once more grabbing hold of his .9, holding the barrel on the weeping Russian, thumbing back the hammer. “Do it, or die now.”

“Then you won’t have sample,” the goon exclaims.

“Oh, I can grab a sample up until five minutes after you’re deceased. Little known fact about dead men. The junk can produce sperm while the body is still warm.” Reaching back into his bag with his free hand. “Only difference is I’ll have to cut it out, which means immediate and total castration.”

Now the Russian goes from purple to red. He also stops crying, as if he’s just wept his last tear. He sits up, wincing in pain. Then sucking in a single deep breath, he unbuckles his pants, pulls them down around his knees and rolls over on top of Sissy.

“May the good Lord forgive me,” he says, as he makes the sign of the cross, then shifts himself forward to go to work on her body.

“May the devil have mercy on your soul, Alexander Stalin,” Georgie says while I step back from the open doors and look the other way.

Chapter 42

IT TAKES LESS THAN five minutes for Alex to give us, and Sissy, the sample we need. He then buckles his pants back up. Georgie helps him out of the van where he proceeds to puke. When he's finished, Georgie and I act as his crutches and lead him back into the house. Inside we find Roger and Suzanne are still holding guns on the seated, wounded Russians. Their blood has collected to form a pool of crimson that covers the floor underneath the chairs.

"What do we do with my house guests, Moonlight?" Roger inquires. He's got an open beer in his free hand. Meanwhile, Suzanne is sitting on the long leather couch, her pistol set on the cushion beside her now that the two Russians are passed out from blood loss and on their way to being dead.

Georgie and I drop Alexander to the floor. With all the Viagra he's ingested, his erection is pup-tenting out of his pants. My guess is he'll carry that wood for forty-eight hours or more.

"We need to call the police," I say.

Georgie nods.

"It's about that time, Moon. Call the cops from the car while we're trucking Sissy back to the morgue."

I ask Roger how he feels about involving the cops at this point.

"If it means these Russians will no longer be up my ass for one million bucks," he says, "I'm ready. I'll even wait here for them."

"What will you tell them, Rog?" I ask.

"The truth," he says, taking a drink of beer. "At least, my version of the truth. I drove back to the house and let myself in. These guys were here waiting for me. Turns out Sissy had some illegal drug dealings with them and now they wanted their money. Now that Sissy's gone they wanted me to pay. They pulled their guns on me, but I was able to get the jump on them. I shot them in self-defense. Just like the first time around when I shot that man for trespassing."

"We've got three different caliber of bullets embedded into these Russian's legs and into the woodwork," Georgie points out. "How is Roger going to explain that?"

I start wracking my brain for an answer when the bullet wizzes past my right ear.

Chapter 43

I HIT THE FLOOR.

So does Georgie and Roger.

Suzanne slides off the couch, crawls around the back of it. Alexander crawls over to Roger, snatches the .44 Magnum from his hand, cold-cocks the author over the head with the barrel.

Another couple of rounds tear through the windows and into the floor at my feet.

Alexander raises up the gun, fires one off at Georgie. The bullet misses and takes a chunk out of the wall behind him.

Georgie rolls in my direction, pulling out his .9mm, aiming it at Alexander, and proceeds to pump three rounds into his head.

No more Alexander.

Coming from outside the now shot through windows are the sounds of boot heels on the wood desk and an ear-piercing screech. Correction. Not a screech at all, but a good old-fashioned rebel yell. Then comes the sound of the kitchen door being kicked in. In steps two men and behind them two women.

"Git yer asses down on the floor," screams the short, chubby redneck, his bolt-action 30.06 hunting rifle gripped in both his hands.

"We're already on the floors you morons," Georgie yells, his right hand still gripping his .9mm.

"We got us here the Richard 'Dick' Moonlight," screeches the tall, bearded one, a double-barreled shotgun aimed at the ready. "Wanted for the murder of Missus Sissy Walls."

"Let me guess, Harlan," I say from down on the floor, still on my stomach. "You aims to turn my hide in to the law."

"That's exactly what we're going to do," says the woman standing behind him. "Unless, of course, we negotiate a little settlement. Out of court so to speak." The woman giggles, like she's having a lot of fun. The woman beside her giggles too. The giggles sound identical, since the women are identical twins.

I know one of them. But from down on the floor, I'm not entirely sure which one I know, since they are dressed in the same clothing. Tall leather boots over knee-high socks and short white, thigh-length dresses with pleasant flower prints on them. Aviator sunglasses conceal their eyes and the way they wear their clean and conditioned brown hair parted neatly over their left eye brings out the whiteness in their perfect teeth.

"Erica," I say, "perhaps you should introduce us all to your twin sister."

Chapter 44

"SO WHAT IS IT you girls want?" I say, knowing that if we don't get Sissy's body back to the morgue in less than an hour, I will not only be wanted for murder, but also body snatching.

"I don't know," says the one who is now obviously Erica to her twin. "What exactly do we want, Vanessa?"

"We don't need any money," Vanessa says. "We got lots of that now. Thanks to Roger and his booze."

I steal a glance at the author. He's still passed out from the pistol whipping Alexander Stalin gave him. He's mumbling in his sleep. Something about wanting another round for everyone. He's buying.

"You took Roger's money," I say. "The million the Russians put up. You must have both been present when Roger went to the train station for the payoff. One of you sits at the table with Roger and when he got up to take a leak, the other simply walked away with the bag."

"Yeah but how did you guys even know enough to be there when the drop was supposed to go down?" Georgie poses.

That's when something interesting happens.

Suzanne stands up from behind the couch, stuffs the barrel of the gun she's been holding into the waist of her jeans and approaches the two girls, kissing both of them lovingly on the mouth.

"Because I told them to, Dr. Phillips."

I feel my insides heating up. If only one of those rednecks weren't holding a hunting rifle on me, I'd jump up and tackle all three of them.

"You told them," I say. "Good going, Suzanne. First stealing Brando's manuscript. Then selling drugs. Then stealing a million dollars in cash from some Russian goons. I haven't even asked you about paying my bill."

"Actually, Moonlight," Suzanne says, lighting a cigarette, "the drug running came after I stole the million."

"We stole the million," Erica chimes in.

"Yes, *we*," adds Vanessa. The both of them have these Pepsodent smiles on their faces that tells me that their little life of crime is the most fun they can have with their clothes on.

"Be serious, Moonlight," Suzanne says. "My career wasn't just in the crapper. It was in the sewer. Do you really think the one client I had left was going to pull me out of it? Not only is Roger Walls still suffering from a ten-year-old writer's block, but there isn't a publisher who will touch him even with your dick, Dick."

"Thanks for that little comment," I say.

Behind me, Roger mumbles in his sleep. *"More shots . . . More shots."*

"So why did you hire me to find him?"

"Because I needed him for my newest clients. My new clients who would provide me with the homerun I need to get myself back on top."

"The clients are standing behind you, am I right?" Moonlight the deductive.

Suzanne smokes, glances at each one of the girls.

"Just look at them, Moonlight," she says. "Beauty, sexiness, brains, youth, and a one hell of a book idea."

"Which is?" Georgie poses.

"A project called *Seducing Roger Walls*," she says thought an exhale of blue smoke. "This wouldn't be just a book, but it would be an entire multi-media package. An e-book that links to real video clips of the girls messing with Roger. Having sex with him, stealing his money, following him. The project would be packaged for a reality television series and even have a video game developed. It would make millions."

"I thought you were going to make millions on the Russian project?"

Suzanne laughs.

"Oh how naïve you are, Moonlight. Those Russians weren't going to influence anyone, even if they did manage to put a gun to some poor editor's head. I lied to Alexander. I told him a book about Stalin's great-grandson being a Russian mobster was a sure thing just so I could get some money out of him. I never dreamed we'd get a full million even from them, but there you have it."

"You had no intention of sharing it with Roger, did you?"

Suzanne goes wide-eyed.

"Wow, Moonlight, it's amazing just how swift a private detective you really are."

"What was all that bullshit about getting threatening phone calls from someone who wanted payback? That someone probably being Ian Brando?"

"I just did that to make the story more dramatic and to tweak your curiosity. I knew you'd go back home and Google me and see what I'd done by stealing Brando's piece-of-crap book, and that alone would keep you in the game, keep you asking questions, keep you getting into trouble, keep you making a richer, more in depth and plot-driven story for me and the girls. You see, Moonlight, a book isn't just a book. In the end, a book should entertain, don't you agree?"

Vanessa pulls a phone from the chest pocket on her vest.

"Smile, Moonlight," she says. "You're on *Candid Camera*."

Georgie rises up onto his knees.

"Get the hell back down, skinny," Tall Redneck shouts.

"Oh fuck you, you dumb ass Okie," Georgie says. "Go ahead and shoot."

Short Round Redneck raises up his rifle, fires. The bullet hits the wall behind Georgie. I rise up onto my knees, take a look at Georgie's face. It's tight and red. I've known him nearly my whole life and I know when he's scathing mad. Like now, as he raises up his .9mm while thumbing back the hammer.

"Don't do it!" screams Short Round Redneck as he aims for Georgie's head.

I get ready to spring myself in the direction of the Rednecks when a second shot rings out and a body drops.

Chapter 45

SHORT ROUND REDNECK'S FACE disappears a split second before his body hits the kitchen floor.

The twins drop down onto their stomachs and scream like spoiled brats.

Suzanne pulls out her gun, aims it at me.

Why me?

I reach out, grab the .44 as a shot is fired and brushes the short hair on my head. Raising up the Magnum, I fire at Suzanne, and hit her in the chest. She's gone before her knees even begin to buckle.

I just killed the world's best literary agent.

That's when the canister of tear gas plops onto the floor by my feet and explodes.

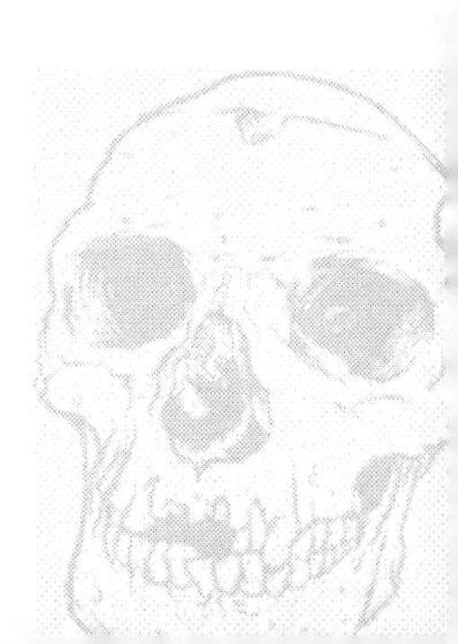

Chapter 46

THE TEAR GAS IS followed by an entire SWAT team that plows through the busted windows and broken doors. I try and cover my eyes to prevent the gas from stinging them, but it's a futile effort. I can hear Georgie coughing up a lung, along with Tall Bearded Redneck. The twins are still down on the ground. They've gone from screaming to outright weeping and wailing. They've become victims in their own little game of seduction. As for the two Russians duct-taped to one another, they aren't making a sound. Maybe they're dead.

One of the SWAT officers bends over, looks me in the eye with his oxygen-masked and clear-shielded face. "You okay, buddy?"

I nod.

He holds out his arm and points to the open door of the kitchen. "Go!" he demands. Then at Georgie. "You too, Dr. Phillips!"

I go for the door, Georgie on my tail.

Outside, I cough and weep, weep and cough.

It takes a couple of minutes for the tears to stop falling and my breathing to return to some semblance of normal. When I can finally see straight, I spot Detective Miller making his way through the throngs of cop cars, EMT vans, and a couple of black armored SWAT vehicles. There's a woman walking beside him. She's tall, slim, wearing a windbreaker and jeans. Even with my tear-gassed eyes still stinging and somewhat blurred, I can tell she's crying. Or has been crying anyway.

Miller directs me to a place on the lawn that isn't in earshot of the police or anyone else, but that is in plain eyesight of the van containing Sissy's body.

"How'd you know we'd be here?" I say after a time.

"I'm a cop, Moonlight," he says. "Didn't take a whole lot of deductive reasoning once we found out that Sissy was missing from the morgue." Then turning to the woman. "And I had some help from Erica and Vanessa's mother. Moonlight, meet Mrs. Alice Beckett."

"Pleased to meet you," I say. "Pardon me if I don't shake your hand."

"No worries," the sixty-something, gray-haired woman says in a soft, low voice.

"Mrs. Beckett has been aware for some time the arrangement her daughters struck up with Suzanne Bonchance for the publication of their book project. But it wasn't until Sissy died that she uncovered the extent of the illegalities involved."

"Ms. Beckett," I say, my still stinging eyes planted on Georgie's van, and the now closed back-bay doors. "Did your daughter's kill Sissy?"

The woman starts to cry again. In her right hand, she's holding a cloth handkerchief. As quickly as the tears fall from her eyes onto her flush cheeks, she wipes them away.

"I overheard Vanessa talking to Erica on the phone last night from the kitchen in my home. Vanessa was upset. She was crying.

Sometimes shouting, sometimes whispering. But crying. She had done something. Something bad. Something she didn't mean to do." Beckett takes a moment to dry more of her tears. "And then she said the name, Sissy. In the same breath, my daughter said the word dead. That Sissy was dead, and it was all a big mistake."

"Sissy didn't OD on her own?" I say, wiping my own tear-gas produced tears from my face.

"She had . . . let's call it . . . assistance," Miller says.

My eyes back on Beckett.

"My Vanessa did something bad to the drugs."

Miller takes a step forward.

"Vanessa laced the drugs with something. Heroin. She must have gotten it from Suzanne. Suzanne from the Russians. By now you've no doubt figured out the food chain in this thing, Moonlight."

"Why would she do that?" I say. "Why take a chance on killing Sissy?"

"The girls were playing a game of manipulation. It was pure fun for them. Tease Roger and see what happens. Follow him, see what happens. Take him to bed, see what happens. Steal his money or, in this case, the Russian's money. Haunt him so that he can't write even if he tries. See what happens. Get it all on video at the same time. Write a book about it. Strut your twin tits and ass. Smile a lot. Say funny, mindless things. Make a fortune."

"You knew about all this, Mrs. Beckett?"

She nods, sniffles. "Some of it. A lot of it. It's been hard for me to pay attention to the girls since my husband left me a half dozen years ago. Does that make me an accomplice in a murder?"

I can't help but recall Erica (or was it Vanessa?) telling me how her mother and father, childhood brides and parents that they were, were still happily together after all these years.

"It's possible Sissy had an existing heart condition," Miller adds. "Anyway, she overdosed on a drug she didn't realize she was ingesting."

A uniformed police officer approaches us.

"Excuse me, Detective," he says, handing Miller an iPhone. The same iPhone Vanessa held up inside the kitchen of the Walls home and announced, *"Smile, you're on* Candid Camera*."* He thumbs a few commands until he comes to the application he wants. He holds the phone at an angle that allows Ms. Beckett and myself to see the screen. It's a video. He depresses the triangular play button. It's Sissy, lying in bed, naked. She's snorting a line from the mirror. She's singing and slurring her words. Some Lindsay Lohan song. Her eyes are going in and out of focus while Vanessa zooms in on them.

"Do you love your husband, Sissy?" Vanessa asks.

Sissy issues a laugh. A long drawn out, pain-filled exhale that is as far away from happiness as hell is from paradise.

"I want to die when I hear his name," she says, grabbing hold of a beer bottle she has set on the night stand, spilling half of it before she can get it to her mouth. She's not finished taking her drink, when the bottle falls onto her lap, spilling out in a sea of white foam. Her eyes roll up into the back of her head and her mouth begins to froth, her body cascading into a fit of trembling.

"Oh shit! Oh shit!" Vanessa can be heard saying while she continues filming. "Shit. Fuck me. Sissy. Don't die. Sissy don't die."

But it's plain to see, that the eighth wife of Roger Walls is already gone.

Miller stops the video. "She must have filmed the whole thing," he says. "She wanted to see what happened next instead of calling for help." He shakes his head and pockets the phone.

Just then we see the girls being led out of the house, both of their wrists handcuffed behind their backs, their hair veiling their tear-gassed faces like funeral shawls.

Ms. Beckett begins to openly sob, while Miller begins making his way back across the side lawn to where they are being led to an awaiting police cruiser. Not knowing what else to do, I follow. When he comes to within a few feet of them, the tall, short-haired detective shoves his hands in his jacket pockets, pulls out a pack of cigarettes. He pops one between his lips and lights it with a *BIC* butane.

The same uniformed cop who handed Miller the iPhone opens the back cruiser door for Erica. He places his open hand on her head and pushes down on it so that she doesn't get smacked on the door rim as she enters into the vehicle. He does the same thing for Vanessa when she slips into the car beside her twin sister.

When the girls are safely inside the car, Miller reaches out with his free hand, grabs hold of the car door in order to prevent the cop from closing it. The detective, cigarette pressed between his lips, leans his head into the car. He says something to the girls which is indiscernible to me. They respond with an answer, which is just as indiscernible. Popping his head back out, he tells the cop to take them away.

Turning to the girl's mother, he says, "Mrs. Beckett, you can follow them in one of the other cruisers. The officer here will assist you." He gives me a look, and together we walk back across the lawn to Georgie's van.

Chapter 47

WE STAND BY THE white van in heavy silence, my eyes no longer burning or tearing. Miller reaches back into his blazer pocket, produces that same pack of smokes. Marlboro Lights. My brand it so happens. He offers me one and since my life hangs in the balance anyway, I accept it. He fires it up for me and for a few long moments, we just stand there smoking to the soundtrack of arguing cops, busy EMTs, tinny radios, ringing cell phones. Even laughter.

"Do I dare ask you what you wanted with Sissy's body, Moonlight?" Miller speaks after a time.

"I think you know why."

"DNA."

"Yup."

He smokes. Contemplatively.

"Georgie Phillips. He cleaned her out. So to speak."

I smoke. Reflectively.

"So to speak."

"Perhaps you replaced the sample with another. Thus the reason for bringing her on this field trip."

"All things are possible."

"Will the DNA we find inside her match that of a living human being?"

I smoke a little more, exhale. "Do we ever really die, Detective?"

He shakes his head. "If you deliver her body back to the Albany Medical Center within the hour, I will make certain no one is the wiser. But it has to be within the hour."

"Understood. Why you being so nice?"

He flicks the half-smoked cigarette onto the gravel drive, where it lands and smolders in the fresh oxygen.

"You've helped me out. Helped your fellow man out, I should say. Whether you realize it or not, Moonlight, you've helped bust up a Russian mob-run coke operation and did away with one of their operatives and seriously wounded two of their soldiers. It's too bad Suzanne Bonchance had to die, but I understand you were acting in self-defense. You were a cop once. You were trained when to shoot and when not to."

"I don't like taking lives, even when they're trying to take mine. But it always seems to happen."

"One day when you least expect, your life will be taken too."

"Sudden death. It's something I have to live with."

"Ain't that the truth," Miller says. Then, tossing a thumb over his shoulder at the van and the body it contains. "Within the hour. I mean it, Moonlight. Or all bets are off."

"Roger that, Detective."

He steps past me and begins making his way around the back of the house. Until I call out for him, stopping him. He turns.

"What is it?"

"What did you say to the twins back there inside the cruiser? Or you don't have to tell me if you don't want to."

He nods, runs his right hand through his closely cropped, sandy blond hair.

"It's okay," he says. "I don't mind."

"So what did you say then?"

"I asked them why they did it? Why they tried to ruin Roger's life?"

"And what did they say?"

"They said it was fun."

I flick away what's left of my cigarette so that it lands on the gravel drive not far from the detective's. "It was fun? That's it?"

"Oh, and they also said he deserved it, for what he did to their mom thirty-seven some years ago."

I picture a destroyed Mrs. Beckett. Picture her crying all the way to the Albany Police Department in the back of some wormy smelling cruiser. My pulse picks up a little at the thought of she and Walls somehow coming together three decades ago.

"What did he do?"

"He slept with her while visiting her college in Boston for a reading. Got her pregnant. She was forced to give up the child."

"Did she ever connect with the child later on?"

"Yup. But Roger never did. Rather, Roger has no idea who his own son is. But I have a feeling now might be the time for him to find out, once and for all."

He stands there staring at me.

"Well don't keep me in the dark, Miller."

He tells me the name of Roger Walls long-lost son, and Erica and Vanessa Beckett's older, half brother. And it all makes perfect sense.

Chapter 48

PROFESSOR OATCZUK WILL PROBABLY be pleased to know that he is the proud offspring of one of the world's most gifted writers. Or maybe he already knows. Maybe he's known for a long time and that's why he portends such a sentimental affinity to someone who didn't seem all that nice to him. But it would explain why he wanted to work with Suzanne so badly, and why he refused to even consider working with another agent. If he's known all along that Roger is his true father, he would want to make his dad proud. It would be a way for Oatczuk to be noticed, to be praised, to be a success in his daddy's eyes, even if said daddy had no way of knowing the writing prof was his long-lost son.

I can only wonder if Oatczuk knew about his true connection to Erica and Vanessa. Has he known for some time that he is their half-brother? That they share the same mother? Or did Alice Beckett manage to keep the lid on the complicated family secret until very recently? As recently as today? As recently as this very hour?

If I have to guess, I would say the truth about Roger and his sisters has only now been revealed, while the truth about his biological father was revealed a long time I ago. Why he never confronted the bestseller with the truth, I'll never know, but I can bet it has something to do with being his own man. After all, who really wants to be the kid of a superstar novelist like Roger Walls? Who wants to be buried in his wake? Who really needs the pressure of measuring up? Measuring up as both a writer and a man? A man's man?

My spell is broken by the sound of shouting.

"Give that back you son of a philandering bastard!" barks Roger Walls. He's chasing Georgie Phillips halfway across the lawn towards the van. Georgie has a bottle of Jack Daniels gripped in his hand by its neck.

"Don't just stand there, Moon!" the pathologist screams. "Help me!"

I run, jump in between them, praying that Roger doesn't mow me down like a Sherman tank and a dandelion.

"What's going on?" I ask, grabbing hold of Roger's thick right arm, trying to hold him back with both my hands.

"That thief has stolen my whiskey!" Roger shouts.

Georgie stands by the van, panting, the bottle of whiskey still held tightly in his hand.

"Listen Moon," he says, "our literary friend here is suffering from loose lips. He's babbling on about my little secret arrangement at the AMC morgue. Before he got too far, I made like a rabbit and stole his drink right out from under him. I knew he'd give chase if so provoked."

"And here we are, asshole. Now give it back."

"Boys, boys," I say. "No one calls the other an asshole." Me, turning back to Roger, looking him in the eyes. "Roger apologize to Georgie."

Roger just stands there, panting.

I turn to Georgie, while holding back Roger.

"Georgie, hand him back his booze."

Georgie does it. Roger uncaps it, takes a deep drink.

"That's more like it. Sorry I called you an asshole, Doc. But getting in between a man and his booze is a dangerous business."

"There's another reason I took that bottle, Roger," Georgie says. "I love your books, man. I'm a real fan. And you know how many diseased livers I've examined in my life by men who would have lived another twenty productive years if they just decided to slow down a little? I just want the big guy here to keep on living and to write the great books I know he's got in him."

Roger stands there in shock, the bottle gripped in his hands.

"Georgie," he says, "that's one of the nicest things anyone has ever said to me." Lifting the bottle of Jack, he stares into it. For split second I think he's about to toss it to the pavement. But instead, he takes another sip, and passes it on to me. "Have a shot, Moonlight. You look like you just lost your best friend."

I take hold of the bottle and steal a drink. I'd pass the bottle to Georgie, but he's already rolling a joint and both his hands are occupied. I can't say everything is back to normal. Not by a long shot, but I can tell the worst of this train wreck is over. Now all that has to be done is to return Sissy to the morgue. Which is what I convey to Georgie in detail.

"Then we'd better get a move on," he says, inhaling a major hit of his medicinal weed.

"Mind if I get a hit of that?" Roger says.

"Inside the van," I insist. "You're going to need it after the news I'm about to lay on you."

"News," Roger says, climbing into the van's shotgun seat. "What news?"

"You're going to be a daddy, Roger."

Georgie turns over the engine and together, the three of us along with one dead body begin making our way back to Albany.

Epilogue

WE SIT AROUND THE table in the 677 Prime steakhouse like one big happy family. Me, Roger Walls, and his lost-but-now-found son, Gregor Oatczuk. A fourth person chooses to stand while he raises up a glass of champagne to make a toast.

"Here's to my newest powerhouse authors," states literary agent William Craig Williams. "Congratulations on your present successes and your good fortune to come."

"Yeah, yeah, Willy," Roger laughs, taking a drink of beer from the open bottle of Bud set before him. "Like you won't hesitate to drop one of us if we stop moving units. Sit your ass down before you embarrass us. And order more of those jumbo shrimp."

Williams sits down and pours more champagne all around. He's smiling and pretending to be good humored despite Roger's assessment of literary disloyalty. But the agent has reason to celebrate. He's not only succeeded at acquiring Roger a new three-book deal with one of the biggest houses in the land, he was also able to secure a tidy mid-six figure sum for an advance. He also sold Oatczuk's, a.k.a. Ian Brando's, most recent opus *Dancing with the Dead*, for an equal sum. He even sold *Moonlight Falls* for a nice advance that will keep me in food and beer for a year or more.

I feel kind of like a star being included in the company of real writers. Makes me feel kind of special. But I'm not about to give up my day job. Turns out private detecting is not only a good way to make some money, it's also a way to come up with a plot for the new book I'm now contracted to write as the follow-up to *Moonlight Falls*.

Who'd ever have guessed: Richard "Dick" Moonlight. Captain Head-Case and author.

"Tell me, Gregor," I say, after a time, "why did you decide to send you manuscript to Suzanne Bonchance under a pen name?"

He sips some champagne, sets the glass down, runs his hand over his trim black beard. A beard that now makes him look a lot like his father.

"I knew that she wouldn't like it simply because she didn't like any of the other books I'd sent her. She was clouded by poor judgment. I knew I had a good book and I wanted her to see not the name Oatczuk, but something hip and fresh. Turns out she really liked the story."

"A little too much," Roger adds. "She stole it. Thus began her downfall and the long and lurid tale that would climax with her death in the kitchen of my former Chatham home. A tale that you no doubt will be writing sooner than later, am I right Moonlight?"

"Do you have a title yet, Richard?" begs William.

"I'm thinking *Moonlight Sonata*," I say.

"Has a good ring to it if I don't say so myself," Roger says, drinking down the rest of his beer, then holding up his hand to grab the waiter's attention.

The talk and back-talk goes on like that for a while, everyone getting drunker, the mood getting lighter, William Craig Williams growing more enthusiastic about selling our movie and foreign rights. We talk about world tours, reviews in *People Magazine*, and about *Moonlight Falls* being a great vehicle for Clooney or Pitt. Williams makes real and mental notes and after a time, I simply tune out and fade away into the back of my own mind. Is this it? Is this what it's all about? The literary life?

After a while I stand and excuse myself from the table.

"I need to make a phone call," I say, and head back across the dining room to the restaurant's front door. Stepping outside into the warm, moonlit night, I pull a cigarette from the pack inside my leather coat, and fire it up. I retrieve my cell phone from my pocket and speed-dial my son in Los Angeles. I wait for the connection while I listen to the rings over the sound of my pulse beating in my temples. When the connection is made, I hear the machine click on.

"You've reached the home of Lynn and Harrison Harder, please leave a message at the tone and have yourself a great day."

I wait for the beep and when it comes I am left only with silence and nothing to say. I draw a complete blank. Me, the new author. The man of words. I can't even work up a simple hello or I love you for my son. Instead I thumb End and stuff the phone back into my coat pocket.

When did Lynn drop Bear's last name for her own maiden name? She never consulted me about it. But then, I suppose she considers herself much more of a father to our son than I am. But she has no idea how much I miss the little guy and what I wouldn't do to get him back. Maybe now that I have a new writing job to go with my day job, I can afford to bring him back to Albany for a while.

I smoke and gaze through the windows into the restaurant.

I see my table and the men who occupy it, minus myself. Roger is holding court. He's got a napkin draped over his head and he's holding the champagne bottle by its neck. His son Gregor is laughing hysterically as is William Craig Williams and quite a few admirers who occupy the surrounding tables.

Roger Walls, local celebrity author. I found him and found out a lot more about myself in the process.

Tossing my cigarette to the macadam, I stamp it out. I begin making my way back to the front entrance. But I don't get half way before something stops me. I turn and begin walking the opposite way, back toward the downtown and the colorful neon that lights up the juke joints and the dancehalls on lower Broadway, not far from my riverside loft where I live alone.

Pulling up the collar on my leather coat, I decide to walk away from it all to the sound of a heart that beats under a cover of brilliant moonlight.

ACKNOWLEDGEMENTS

TWO GREAT WRITERS PROVIDED me with the inspiration for the character of Roger Walls. The first is the real-life Roger Walls, who was as gifted a poet as he was a loyal friend to me during our time together at writing school. There hasn't been a day that's gone by since his passing that I don't think of him. The second is hard-boiled genius, James Crumley, whom I never got to meet, but if I had, I'm sure he would have let me buy him a beer or two in the dark juke joint of his choosing.

VZ
New York, NY
July 12, 2013

ABOUT THE AUTHOR

VINCENT ZANDRI IS THE No. 1 International Bestselling Amazon author of THE INNOCENT, GODCHILD, THE REMAINS, MOONLIGHT FALLS, THE CONCRETE PEARL, MOONLIGHT RISES, SCREAM CATCHER, BLUE MOONLIGHT, MURDER BY MOONLIGHT, THE GUILTY, MOONLIGHT SONATA, CHASE, and more. He is also the author of the Amazon bestselling digital shorts, PATHOLOGICAL, TRUE STORIES and MOONLIGHT MAFIA. Harlan Coben has described THE INNOCENT (formerly As Catch Can) as ". . . gritty, fast-paced, lyrical and haunting," while the New York Post called it "Sensational . . . Masterful . . . Brilliant!" Zandri's publishers include Delacorte, Dell, StoneHouse Ink, StoneGate Ink, and Thomas & Mercer. An MFA in Writing and graduate of Vermont College, Zandri's work is translated into many languages including Dutch, Russian, and Japanese. An adventurer, foreign correspondent, and freelance photo-journalist for Living Ready, RT, Globalspec, as well as several other news agencies and publications, Zandri lives in New York. For more visit www.vincentzandri.com

Made in the USA
Lexington, KY
06 February 2014